Dear America

The Diary of
Piper Davis

The Fences
Between Us

KIRBY LARSON

SCHOLASTIC INC. • NEW YORK

This book is dedicated to all of the nearly 120,000 Americans of Japanese descent who were incarcerated in the ten War Relocation Camps during World War II, but especially to those in Minidoka.

Library of Congress Cataloging-in-Publication Data
Larson, Kirby.
The fences between us : the diary of Piper Davis / by Kirby Larson.
p. cm. — (Dear America)
Summary: Thirteen-year-old Piper Davis records in her diary her experiences beginning in December 1941 when her brother joins the Navy, the United States goes to war, she attempts to document her life through photography, and her father — the pastor for a Japanese Baptist Church in Seattle — follows his congregants to an Idaho internment camp, taking her along with him. Includes historical notes. Includes bibliographical references (   ).

Trade Paper-Over-Board edition ISBN 978-0-545-22418-5
Reinforced Library edition ISBN 978-0-545-26232-3

1. World War, 1939–1945 — United States — Juvenile fiction. 2. Japanese Americans — Evacuation and relocation, 1942–1945 — Juvenile fiction. 3. Minidoka Relocation Center — Juvenile fiction. [1. World War, 1939–1945 — United States — Fiction. 2. Japanese Americans — Evacuation and relocation, 1942–1945 — Fiction. 3. Photography — Fiction. 4. Diaries — Fiction.] I. Title.
PZ7.L32394Fe 2010
[Fic] — dc22
2009044972

10 9 8 7 6 5 4 3 2 1   10 11 12 13 14

The text type was set in ITC Legacy Serif.
The display type was set in Savoye.
Book design by Kevin Callahan

Printed in the U.S.A.   23
First edition, September 2010

Seattle,
Washington

1941

Saturday, November 8, 1941

I've never been the diary type, but now I have something to write about.

I didn't think this day would come so soon. The minute he graduated from high school in June, my big brother, Hank, enlisted in the Navy — so he can see the world and that sort of thing. Trixie says she's glad he went Navy because he looks so dreamy in the dark middy and white sailor hat. I think he would've looked just as dreamy in a University of Washington letterman's jacket. That way he could still be home, with us, where he belongs.

Here's what happened when he told us that day. Margie had made some new recipe and we were all picking at it, trying to find the edible bits. I was thinking about calling Trixie to see if she wanted to go for a soda after supper, to celebrate the end of sixth grade. Pop was making notes for a church meeting. Margie was probably daydreaming about her new boyfriend, Stan. All of a sudden, Hank put down his fork.

"So I guess I better tell you guys before I burst." He was wearing a smile even bigger than the one he wore when Garfield won the state baseball championships. "You're looking at Seaman Davis."

"What are you talking about?" Margie froze in her chair.

Hank saluted. "I enlisted. You-Nited States Navy. I'll be on my way to boot camp in a week."

Even though I was almost thirteen I bawled like a baby. I didn't even feel like dessert, and it was lemon meringue pie. Margie got a funny look on her face, but she didn't let on what she was feeling. She's like that. She didn't even cry when she broke her leg skiing that time.

Pop did what he did best. Talked. It comes naturally for a preacher, I guess. Anyway, first he talked about Hank being so young. Hank said eighteen wasn't that young. Then Pop asked him about college. Hank said he'd get an education in the Navy and he'd get to see the world. Then Pop brought up the war in Europe.

"These are troubled times, son. Hitler's on the march in Europe, and heaven only knows what Japan will do after occupying so much of Indochina."

"Those are not our battles, Pop. We're not at war," Hank said.

"But for how long?" Pop shook his head. "For how long?"

That's when Hank lost his temper. He pushed himself back from the table.

"Pop, you've got to let me grow up and make my own decisions. Besides, President Roosevelt promised we weren't going to get involved. It's the peacetime Navy for me, all the way. You can worry about me falling overboard or getting a tattoo or getting seasick. But one thing you do not have to worry about is me being in that war."

Pop didn't say anything for a minute, just stirred another spoonful of sugar into his coffee. And then he said, "You're right, son. This is your decision to make. I may wish you'd made a different one, but I would never change one thing about you. You have grown up into a fine young man."

Well, that got me weepy all over again. Margie said, "I believe we could all use some pie," and that was the end of that.

Pop didn't say much afterward, but all summer long whenever he read anything about what the Germans were doing in Europe or the Japanese in China, he made sure to clip the article out and send it to Hank at boot camp. Me, I sent him jokes.

When he finished boot camp and got his orders, Hank called home. Long distance! No one else was here so I got to take the call. "Tell Pop I got the best assignment ever—Hawaii," he said. "Nothing to worry about there but getting hit in the head by a falling coconut." I screamed and jumped up and down when Hank said he'd get to come home for a whole week before he shipped out for Pearl Harbor.

I've never had a week go by so fast. He spent time with his buddies, sure, but he made time for me, too. We went to the show, went fishing by Ray's Boathouse, and last Sunday morning before church, we had a pancake-eating contest. Hank won, of course.

The worst day of his visit home was today, the day we had to say good-bye. Mrs. Harada came with us to see Hank off. I was only a baby when she started taking care of us. As we stood there on the dock trying to pick Hank out of all the sailors, Mrs. Harada kept saying, "My little boy, my little boy," over and over again. Margie didn't shed a tear, of course, but I cried enough for the both of us put together. I'm not a worrier, like Pop. Besides, Hank can take care of himself. I'm blue because he's the best big brother in the world and I'm going to miss him like the dickens.

I couldn't look at his ship when it pulled out of port. I felt like a little kid—maybe if I didn't look, he wouldn't really be gone—but I didn't care. Mrs. Harada put her arm around my shoulder. Her hugs have helped me feel better after skinned knees or bad scores on spelling tests. But nothing could fill up the Hank-sized hole in my heart.

Then she told me she had something for me. "Here, Piper," she said, handing me this diary. It fit into my hand like it belonged there.

"It's beautiful." I ran my fingertips over the red cover embossed with gold cherry blossoms.

"I bought it a long time ago. I was saving it for the right time." She hugged me. "Now seems like the right time."

"It's the perfect time," Pop said. "Every thirteen-year-old girl could benefit from the self-reflection a diary offers."

I made a face. Leave it to Pop to turn a cheer-up gift into a sermon.

"This is Piper's," said Mrs. Harada. "No one can tell her what to write in it. Not even you." She wagged her finger at Pop.

I liked that idea. Having a place I could write whatever I wanted.

And I want to write that I already miss my brother.

Sunday, November 9, 1941

Boy, oh, boy was Pop's sermon long today. If Hank had been here, we could've written each other notes in our secret code. I don't know how Margie can sit there through the whole thing. She's probably used to it, though, having to sit through all those college Chem lectures.

I wonder how long it will take Hank to get to his base in Pearl Harbor?

I wonder when he'll send me a letter.

I wonder if I'll be able to survive my brother being in the Navy.

Monday, November 10, 1941

It's not fair! I bought that tube of Tangee lipstick with my own money, and Pop won't let me wear it. He wants me to be such a Goody Two-shoes. Trixie says I'm a natural beauty but what else would you expect from a best friend? Margie says to quit moping; I should focus on what's really important in life.

That's easy for her to say. She's got two years of college under her belt and plans to be a pharmacist. Plus a steady boyfriend. I don't have anything like that. I don't even know what I want to do when I grow up!

All I know for sure is that I'm the only girl in seventh grade with naked lips.

Tuesday, November 11, 1941

An airmail letter from Hank! He sent it from San Francisco, on his way to Hawaii. He says everything's going great—he even likes the Navy food. But he does miss our fir trees. What a goof—if I could choose, I'd rather sit under a palm tree than a cedar any day. But it was good to hear from him, even if it made me miss him more.

The last line of Hank's letter was in our code. He wrote: "eritw kacb noos."

So I did!

Saturday, November 15, 1941

Trixie *was* going to come along to help deliver Thanksgiving baskets, until she found out what time we'd be leaving. "On a Saturday morning?" she said. "You know I need my beauty sleep." Trixie's a pal but she says friendship only goes so far! (She was joking.) No sleeping in for me, though. Pop had me up at the crack of dawn to finish filling the baskets.

Betty Sato and her dad were waiting for us at the church. They helped us load up the Blue Box and rode along as we drove through Japantown to pass the baskets out. I noticed that Pop didn't say one word about *her* wearing dungarees even though he didn't allow me to wear mine.

I had more fun last year when it was me and Pop and Hank making the deliveries. Hank cracked jokes and set up challenges, like who could carry a basket on their head the farthest.

Betty isn't the joking-around type. She's the kind of kid all of the adults go crazy over. She plays the piano at church, helps in the Sunday school, and even takes notes on Pop's sermons. Just last night, Pop was reading the church newsletter and said, "I see Betty Sato's made the eighth-grade Honor Roll again." I knew he wondered why my name wasn't ever on that kind of list. I guess I'm not a whiz kid like Margie or Betty.

It's hard to talk over the engine noise so mostly Betty and I just smiled at each other once in a while as we rode around, facing each other on those benches in the back of the Blue Box. I don't know her very well, even though we go to the same church. At school, kids don't mix much. Sometimes I feel like I live in two different worlds: my Sunday world, full of Japanese names and faces, and the rest of the week.

The last stop was Grandma Fujiwara's. We stood around for a long time, shivering, while the grown-ups talked about the war in Europe. "The Nazis are steamrolling over the Russians," Mr. Sato said. "Did you hear they've reached Sevastopol?"

"*Pfft.*" Grandma Fujiwara flapped her hand. "More worried about Japan in China. Not good for any of us," she said.

Pop glanced over at me, then away, quick. I bet he was thinking about Hank. But that was one worry he could cross off his list. Hank was nowhere near any of the fighting. Besides, the U.S. wasn't even in the war.

The grown-ups finished their conversation and

we dropped Betty and her dad off at the church.

We got home in time for me to listen to *Hit Parade*. I liked most of tonight's songs but "Chattanooga Choo-Choo" was my favorite.

Sunday, November 16, 1941

Rain, rain, go away! Pop says even the ducks need umbrellas on days like today!

I told Trixie on Friday that I was keeping a diary. She said that was a good idea because when I'm famous, people will want to read it. I told her I didn't think that was going to happen, but she ignored me and asked me what I named it. I said I hadn't and she got in a dither.

"You have to call it something," she said.

"How about Dear Diary?" I said back.

She rolled her eyes and told me I was hopeless. I don't know what's wrong with Dear Diary. Maybe it could be DeeDee for short? That sounds keen to me, even sophisticated. DeeDee. I like it.

Okay, DeeDee — let me tell you a bit about the person behind the pen (well, sometimes pencil). I'm thirteen, average in looks and intelligence (ask my teachers). I have one sister, one brother, and one parent. That last thing makes me different from most of my friends. My mother died when I was a baby and I honestly don't remember her. Trixie used to ask me if I didn't miss her terribly but how can you miss someone you didn't know? One story about her that I like, though, is that Pop wanted to name me Geraldine, after his favorite aunt, but Margie and Hank wanted to name me Piper. My mother said since she got to pick Hank's name and Pop got to pick Margie's, it was their turn to choose a name. She must've been quite the sweet-talker because Pop went along.

There's not that much more to say about me. I like Sky Bars, big band music, and Bud Greene—who doesn't even know I'm alive.

Monday, November 17, 1941

DeeDee—

Another letter from Hank. He's homesick, of all things. I thought it might help if I sent him some photos of home so I dusted off my old Eastman Kodak and got to work. I'd been crazy about photography in fifth grade—even bought the camera with my own money—but sort of lost interest. It was like meeting up with an old friend when I brought the camera out from the back of my closet. Everything seemed to be in working order but there was only one way to find out. It was between rain showers so I ran outside and took a bunch of pictures — the house, the holly tree in the front yard, and the tree house Hank and I built in the back. I got in quite a few shots before the sky opened up again.

Margie was standing at the stove, stirring the stew. So I got some snaps of her, too. "He might miss being home, but I bet Hank doesn't miss your cooking," I told her. She threw a towel at me, but I kept clicking. I can't figure out why someone who is a whiz at college Chemistry can flop at cooking like she does. I don't complain — much! — because I don't want to get stuck with the job.

The minute I heard Pop pull the Blue Box into the drive, I hurried out to make him pose, too. In his fedora and overcoat, he looked more like Dick Tracy than the minister of the Seattle Japanese Baptist Church. That tickled my funny bone. When I looked through the viewfinder, though, I noticed new circles under Pop's eyes. He works too hard and worries too much.

Tuesday, November 18, 1941

DeeDee —

Hank sent me a photo of him in his uniform. He signed it "Seaman Davis, USS *Arizona*, Ford Island Naval Air Station." I don't know if it's regulation, but he wears his cap set back on his head, with a curly wave of hair in front. With that curl and his Pepsodent smile, Trixie and I both think he looks like a movie star!

He has two new friends from the ship, Del and John. Get this — they're twins. Hank and the twins call themselves the Three Musketeers. On their last liberty, the Three Musketeers dared each other to go swimming on Waikiki Beach, in full uniform, even shoes. Some little kid handed Del a bucket, which he poured over John's head. They took a big bow when they got out, like they were the stars of the show. A bunch of people had gathered around and they were all clapping and laughing and asking to have their photos taken with them. Luckily, it was a hot day and everything dried but their socks by the time they got back to the ship.

Someday, Trixie and I will do something crazy like that. Something worth writing about in this diary!

Wednesday, November 19, 1941

DeeDee —

In homeroom, Myrna Edwards said she had a trade-last for me. The rule about TLs is that I can't hear the compliment she heard about *me* until I tell a compliment I'd heard about *her*. Which is pretty hard to do with Myrna. I fudged, telling her that Donna Murray had said she had nice eyebrows. Donna Murray says nice things about everybody, except maybe Hitler, so that was a safe white lie. Guess what my TL was!? Myrna heard Bud tell Eddy that I could be Maureen O'Sullivan's movie double! Trixie says that proves he's stuck on me. Maybe so. Maybe not.

More letters from Hank today. We each got one and read them aloud after dinner. Hank wrote Pop about going to church in Honolulu and hearing hymns sung in Hawaiian. Margie's told about the USO putting on a luau for the sailors. Hank liked the hula dancing, especially this famous dancer named Hilo Hattie. He even tried poi, which he said is pounded, fermented taro root. He said once was enough and I believe him.

My letter was the best. The Three Musketeers

went to eat at a drive-in called the Kau Kau Korner. They weren't in a car, but that didn't stop them. They acted like they were, "pulling up" right next to one of the speakers where you give your order. The carhop played along, bringing their burgers and malts out and hanging the tray on Hank's arm just like it was a car door. He said people all around them were honking and hooting. What a screwball!

I can't wait to tell Trixie.

Thursday, November 20, 1941 — Thanksgiving

DeeDee —

The dinner table sparkled with Grandma Davis's good china and wedding silver. I took lots of pictures for Hank. I hope they make him feel like he was right here, with us. I sure wish he really was.

After dinner, some friends from church came over for pie. Mrs. Harada brought pumpkin because she knows it's my favorite. The Tokitas brought cherry and old Mrs. Fujiwara brought mincemeat for Pop. Yuck.

Of course Pop had to say grace over the pie, even though we'd already said grace for dinner. "We have much to be thankful for on this day of

Thanksgiving. This delicious food and our dear, good friends. We are especially grateful for Mrs. Fujiwara's continued health, and the blessing of the Tokitas' new baby. This world needs to know your peace and we pray for a quick conclusion to the wars in Europe and China."

"And keep our boy, Hank, safe," Mrs. Harada added.

"Amen," said Pop. Then we all said *amen*.

The grown-ups started talking about the war again. Mr. Harada asked Pop if he'd heard that the Germans had captured Kursk and Yalta. I hurried to our globe to see where those places were. Thankfully, they are halfway around the world from us, in Russia. And from Hank. When I came back in the room, I heard Mr. Harada say, "I hope talks with Japan resume again soon. There's trouble brewing already against us. Did you hear that someone broke the front window at Yoshida's Dry Cleaning?" He shook his head. "The businesses in Japantown have bought over $35,000 of Defense Bonds. That should count for something."

Everyone got very quiet. There had always been some people who had bad feelings about the Japanese living in Seattle, but mostly everyone went about their own business. Since Japan had gone to war against China, things had gotten even harder. But it had been quieter, more on the sly, than breaking a window. Like those awful cartoons in the paper that make Japanese people look like slanty-eyed bucktoothed morons.

To change my mood, I took a picture of Mrs. Tokita and baby Kenji. He is so cute with his button eyes and soft black hair. She let me hold him while she whipped the cream for the pumpkin pie. We played peekaboo and his laugh was better than a bubble bath, washing away all that dreary war talk.

Saturday, November 22, 1941

DeeDee —

Hank's such a card. He sent a list of Navy lingo "so I could impress the boys." Ha! Great joke. Here's some of the lingo:

Admiral's watch: a good night's sleep
Belay: stop it
Bird boat: aircraft carrier
Canary: pretty girl
Fish: torpedo

Mae West: an inflatable life jacket

Monkey drill: calisthenics

Rust bucket: a destroyer, especially an old one,
     or any old boat

Tin can: a destroyer

Hank said he was collecting lots of these but some of them he couldn't share until I was "much older." At the end of the letter, he wrote: "I can tell from those Halloween pictures that my baby sis is growing up to be a real 'canary.'"

Even though it's not true, it's a nice thought. But he has to think that. He's my big brother.

Monday, November 24, 1941

DeeDee —

We finally finished reading *Moby-Dick* in Language Arts. Why do they make us read such boring books? It's pure torture. Miss Wyatt announced a new assignment but said we'd be working in pairs. My ears perked up at that!

Trixie passed me a note: "I'll ask Eddy if you ask Bud!"

I wrote back: "I'm too chicken!"

Right then, Miss Wyatt started asking people who they wanted to partner with. When she called on Bud, he said, "Piper Davis." I nearly fell off my chair.

Miss Wyatt stopped with her pencil over her clipboard. "Piper, is that agreeable to you?"

I was so rattled I said, "Piper. Yes." Like I was talking baby talk. Debbie Sue Wilkins snickered behind me and I wanted to smack her, but when I glanced over at Bud he closed one sparkling green eye in a slow wink.

Pop's always talking about heaven but today I was there!

Tuesday, November 25, 1941

DeeDee —

I can hardly write, my hand's so shaky. Bud walked me home after school! Even carried my books. Trixie said that is absolute proof that he's sweet on me. But, if he is, why did he spend most of the time talking about Hank and the Navy? Sure, I got to use some of that lingo Hank sent me. It didn't seem all that romantic. Boys are a puzzle.

I'll have to ask Trixie about it. She reads all the magazines. All I know is that I've had a crush on

Bud since fifth grade. Oh, those dreamy green eyes. He's droolier than Alan Ladd.

I'm going to write Hank and ask for more Navy stuff!

Bud and I talked about our assignment, which is to write about how the war in Europe is affecting us here. He's going to get home-front facts and I'm going to do man-in-the-hall interviews at school, asking kids what they think. Bud and I make a great team.

While Pop was at his church meeting tonight, I listened to a whole stack of Hank's Bluebird 78s. My favorite is "The Song Is You" — *"I hear music when I look at you."* I wonder if Bud likes it, too. Maybe it could be our song!

Wednesday, November 26, 1941

DeeDee —

Bud walked me home again! And asked if I was going to be at the show on Saturday. It's an Errol Flynn war movie double feature. I'd rather see a romance, but it doesn't matter anyway because Pop won't let me go. He thinks thirteen is too young for dating. He did a whole sermon about it a few months ago. Trixie's parents let her go to the movies with a boy last year, when she was only twelve. Why, oh, why do I have to be a PK?

Maybe if I told Margie I'd do her chores for one whole month, she'd talk to Pop for me. He might listen to her.

Thursday, November 27, 1941

DeeDee —

Al James from homeroom was my first man-in-the-hall interview. He said the war in Europe made him realize how different his life was than for some-one our age in London or Paris or Berlin. "I mean, we worry about whether or not the lunch ladies will make cinnamon rolls and they worry about finding the nearest bomb shelter."

Al's comment made me think about the newsreel I'd seen a few weeks back. A little kid was sitting on a front porch step, after an air raid. But that was all that was left. The front porch step. His house was a pile of rubble. As the camera panned out you could see a woman — maybe his mom — picking through the rubble. She pulled out a crumpled toy truck with only one wheel and gave it to the little boy as the camera zoomed in on his face. He grabbed the truck and held it to his chest but his face didn't change. His expression was empty. As empty as the street behind him.

I'm glad I live here, that's for sure.

Friday, November 28, 1941

DeeDee —

Margie says we girls in love have to stick together. I said I was hardly in love with Bud, but she laughed and said that's what she thought about Stan at first, too. Then she said, "Thirteen's kind of young for true love, but I wonder about twenty. . . ." Her eyes got all misty and I got worried she'd get so wrapped up in daydreaming about Stan that she'd forget about asking Pop for me but she didn't! She not only talked to him, she got him to say yes! I get to go to the show with Bud! And Trixie and Eddy, too, of course.

What if Bud tries to hold my hand?!

I've got to stop biting my nails.

Saturday, November 29, 1941

DeeDee —

Trixie looked so smart in her dungarees, with the cuffs rolled up the way the high school girls do. I felt like an old fuddy-duddy.

"You look really pretty," said Bud. "I like that outfit a lot."

Suddenly, my skirt and blouse felt like they were right out of *Vogue*. I stood up even taller. Bud is a true-blue friend.

Trixie and I sat next to each other, with Eddy by her and Bud by me. Eddy got fresh and put his arm around Trixie's shoulder. Bud was a gentleman through and through. He gave me some of his Jujyfruits but he didn't try to hold my hand. That was lucky because even though I kept wiping it on my skirt, it was slippery as wet soap.

Sure, I'll have pruney hands from doing my chores as well as Margie's, but it will be worth it. This was the best day ever.

Sunday, November 30, 1941

DeeDee —

I helped Mrs. Tokita with her Sunday school class again today. As near as I can tell, with four-year-olds that mostly means washing finger paint out of their hair, keeping crayons out of their mouths, and taking them to the bathroom. We were going to make cinnamon-scented dough ornaments for the church Christmas tree, but one of the boys ate all the dough while we were reading them a Bible story. We did handprint angels, instead.

I wrote Hank about it during the service, signing off, "hisw uoy eerw eerh."

Monday, December 1, 1941

DeeDee —

Bud is so handsome. And so polite. He carried my books *and* made sure he walked on the street side of the sidewalk. I took Trixie's magazine advice this time and asked about his hobbies and interests. He wants to be a fireman like his dad. But if the war doesn't end before he turns eighteen, he'll enlist. In the Marines. I was so busy admiring his dimples that he had to ask me twice what I wanted to do when I was out of high school. I said I didn't really know what I wanted to do but that I liked taking pictures. Do you know what he said? He said, "I can see you as a famous photographer. Maybe working for *Life* magazine." See what I mean?

After supper, I practiced writing "Mrs. Bud Greene" all over my Math homework. I had to start over on a new sheet.

ym tearh selongb ot dub!

Tuesday, December 2, 1941

DeeDee —

In homeroom, I overheard Debbie Sue Wilkins invite Bud to her birthday party. She batted those eyelashes of hers at him and said, "It won't be the same if you don't come." I could tell what his answer was by the big smile he gave her. That's all I needed to see. I dodged him after school and walked home by myself, in the pouring rain, chewing my finger-nails back down to nubbins.

Wednesday, December 3, 1941

DeeDee —

Bud was waiting for me at my locker this morning. He said he does not like Debbie Sue Wilkins, no matter what she tells people.

He walked me home. We held hands for two whole blocks. Well, he walked. I floated. He didn't seem bothered one bit by my bitten-off nails.

erut eovl!

Thursday, December 4, 1941

DeeDee —

Miss Wyatt gave me a few comments on my interview with Al but said I'd done a great job. I've picked Sally West to interview next because her brother's a volunteer with the Flying Tigers, helping to protect the Chinese from Japan.

Later

I wish our neighbor, Mr. Lindstrom, would mind his own beeswax! He saw me holding hands with Bud and told Pop. I got a major lecture about "behavior becoming a young woman." Then he sent me to my room to "think about things."

So here's what I think:

I didn't do anything wrong, but Pop made me feel so guilty. I'll never hold hands with Bud in public again.

I hate nosy neighbors.

I double-hate being a PK.

Saturday, December 6, 1941

DeeDee —

Hank said it's pretty funny to see palm trees strung with Christmas tree lights. But even though there's no chance of a white Christmas in Honolulu, everyone's in the holiday spirit anyway. The Three Musketeers "tinseled" another guy's bunk. He promised to send a photo of it next time.

Reading his letter, it really hit home: He's not going to be here for Christmas. Who will be Santa on Christmas morning? That's always been Hank's job. Who will make the French toast? Who will put the star on the top of the tree?

Pop says it's good to make new traditions.

But I like our old ones just fine.

Sunday, December 7, 1941

While we were at church this morning, Japan attacked Pearl Harbor. It's horrible. Please, God, let Hank be okay.

I've never been so scared in my life. I can't write any more.

Later

I know it's real but it doesn't seem like it can be. How could Japan attack us? *Why?*

Here's what the newsman on the radio just said, "From the NBC newsroom in New York. President Roosevelt said in a statement today that the Japanese have attacked Pearl Harbor, Hawaii, from the air. I'll repeat that. . . . The Japanese have attacked Pearl Harbor, Hawaii, from the air." That's all we know so far. And it's not enough.

Margie made tomato soup and toasted cheese sandwiches for lunch. Pop ate two bites and Margie kept stirring her spoon around and around in her bowl. It's hard to care about food when your stomach is on a pogo stick.

Hank was one of the fastest runners on the baseball team. I couldn't count all the times he'd beat out a throw to first base. But was he fast enough to outrun a Japanese bomber? And where would he run to, there on the ship? I'm curled up on the couch, wrapped tight in the quilt Mrs. Harada made me, shivering as if I were out in the cold.

Margie was at the kitchen table, her Chem book open in front of her, and Pop was in his den, both pretending to work, when we heard those words again: "We interrupt this broadcast to bring you an important bulletin." I ran to the radio and turned up the volume. The report was coming straight from KGU, the Honolulu radio station: "About eight o'clock this morning, Hawaiian time, the first group of Japanese airplanes attacked Ford Island at Pearl Harbor, the Navy's mighty fortress in the islands. . . . Three ships were attacked. The *Oklahoma* was set afire. . . . There has been no statement made by the Navy."

Even though I was under the quilt, my teeth started to chatter. Why weren't they talking about the *Arizona*?

Margie came to sit on the sofa with me. I opened up the quilt so she could crawl under, too. "I want Hank," I said.

She nodded and said, "Me, too."

"Is there room for one more?" Pop asked. We moved over and he wedged between us, his arms around each of our shoulders, holding us tight. We sat that way for a long time.

I leaned my head on his shoulder, his starched shirt scratching my cheek. "You're still in your Sunday clothes," I said.

He looked down at his shirt. "I guess I am." But he didn't move to go change. The radio sucked me in, like a powerful magnet. I couldn't pull myself away. I was terrified of what I might hear but even more terrified not to listen. It was as if my being parked in front of the speaker could somehow make a difference in what happened to Hank.

Margie stood up. "I'll make us some tea."

"Shh." I put my fingers to my lips. "What did they just say?"

Pop reached over and turned up the volume knob. The announcer said, "There will be a complete blackout tonight at eleven o'clock. That blackout is not only for the city of Seattle; it includes every light between the Mexican border and the Canadian border. Every light must be out by eleven o'clock."

"A blackout?" My voice was a little squeak. "Does that mean they think the Japanese might bomb here?" I thought back to Al James's comment. We didn't even have air raid shelters to go to.

"It's a precaution, Piper." Pop slid off the couch and tucked me into the quilt. "You keep listening. Margie and I will get what we need."

But the phone rang right then. It was Mrs. Harada. When Pop hung up, he grabbed his hat and keys. "Piper, you'll have to help Margie. I've got to go." He ran out the door.

I ran after him like some kind of little kid. "Pop! What's wrong?"

"Help Margie," he said, swinging open the driver's door to the Blue Box. "I'll be back as soon as I can."

Margie rummaged around in the basement for something to put on the windows. I got some old blankets from the attic. We didn't talk much while we worked. I wondered if she was straining to listen for enemy planes flying overhead, like I was.

I went right back to my post in front of the radio when we were done. The announcer said that all of the Seattle radio stations were going off the air at 7 P.M., as a precaution. "A precaution for what?" I asked.

"They need to keep the airwaves clear for really

important stuff," Margie said in her matter-of-fact scientist voice.

"But telling us what's happening is really important," I said. What other surprise attacks had Japan planned? What if they came while Pop was gone? I didn't say any of these things out loud, but swallowed them down with a sip of the chamomile tea Margie made us.

The tea grew cold in our cups as we sat in the quiet, listening to the cuckoo clock tick, listening for enemy planes, while we waited for Pop, waited for morning.

Monday, December 8, 1941

DeeDee —

Pop was at the kitchen table, reading the paper, when I got up. WAR DECLARED! blared the headline. From the living room, I could hear the low mumble of the radio. Pop didn't answer when I asked if there was any news about the *Arizona* that morning. His face was about the same color as the oatmeal he wasn't eating.

I read the paper over his shoulder. The *Oklahoma* had been sunk. That was definite. I read the whole front page. Twice. There was not one lick of news about any of the other ships. Not about the *Arizona*.

Margie was already dressed for classes. She made some toast and set it in front of me. A blob of unmelted butter slid around the toast, like a sinking ship, then slowly melted into the bread. I pushed the plate away from me.

"You need to eat something." Margie stood over me while I took a bite. It was harder to chew than a piece of beef gristle but I finally got it swallowed. The minute it hit my stomach, it began pushing its way back up.

"I've got to get back over to the church this morning," Pop said. "Shall I drive you to school?"

"School?" My brother was missing in a horrible sneak attack and Pop was expecting me to go to school?

"It won't do any good to sit around, Piper." Pop finished his coffee. "Not for you nor for Hank."

A tear dribbled down my cheek when I heard him say Hank's name. All night long, even after Pop got home, tight-lipped about why he'd left, I'd lain awake, worrying. There were lots of ships docked in Pearl Harbor, weren't there? Lots of other targets besides the *Arizona*. I had refused to let myself think any bad thoughts. I had prayed harder than I'd prayed in a long time. When I asked Pop if he thought we'd hear anything today, he shook his head. "I don't know, Piper. I just don't know."

That's when I heard a funny noise. It was Margie. At first I thought she had the hiccups. But one look at her scrunched-up face told me she was trying to hold back a sob. Pop and I stared at the table, each of us pretending we hadn't heard.

After a few seconds, she was okay again, buttoning up her coat like nothing had happened, like this was any ordinary day and not a day when we'd just gotten into a war and our brother was bombed.

Seeing Margie all broken up made me ice-cold scared — for Hank and for us, too. That fear sent me crawling onto Pop's lap like I was a little kid. I bawled all over his freshly ironed shirt. One thing about Pop — when you really, really need him, he's there for you. He patted my back until I was cried out. Sniffling, I started to wipe my nose with my bathrobe sleeve. Pop handed me his clean handkerchief and said I might want to go wash my face.

When I slid off his lap, I noticed how tired he

looked. I'd heard him come in close to three; we'd just said "good night" to each other. "I didn't hear last night. What's wrong at the Haradas'? Is Grandmother Harada sick?"

"No one's sick there." He took off his glasses and rubbed his eyes. "We'll talk about it later. It's time to get ready for school or you'll be late."

I washed my face in cold water until the red blotches around my eyes and mouth were gone. I grabbed a skirt and sweater from my closet without looking to see if they matched. Pop's handkerchief went in my pocketbook, in case more tears tried to escape later in the day. I didn't care if I was late. I needed to walk today. Needed the fresh air. Pop said he understood.

The streets were silent and somber. It seemed as if our whole neighborhood were holding its breath, wondering what might happen next. After a few blocks, my ears ached with the cold. I realized I'd forgotten my muffler and hat. It was good to feel something somewhere; I'd been numb since first hearing the news of the attack.

Ahead of me, about a block from school, I saw Betty Sato. Her head was tucked down like she was pushing herself forward against a heavy wind.

As she started up the front steps to the school, some eighth-grade boys—I don't know who they were—stepped into a circle around her. I kept walking, my knees wobbling, right past their huddle on the stairs.

"Dirty Jap!" one boy said.

"We don't want you here," said another.

Then I heard the unmistakable sound of someone spitting. I turned and saw Betty's hand go to her face.

I couldn't say anything. Couldn't do anything. I didn't even give her the hanky in my pocketbook so she could wipe that gob of spit off her face. If I had stopped to help—well, what would those boys have thought? From the outside, it probably looked like I was walking to homeroom as I always did, as if it were a normal, ordinary school day. But inside, I was shaky and sick and mixed-up.

Our principal, Miss Mahon, called an assembly this morning. I always thought she was a tough old battle-ax but her voice quivered as she talked. She said that though we may not all look the same, we are all American citizens and citizens treat one another with respect. Sitting there, listening to her, my stomach hurt even worse as I thought about

Hank and Pearl Harbor. I barely made it to the girls' room before I lost my breakfast. I rinsed out my mouth and washed my face again, but didn't feel any better.

I remembered one time when I was in first or second grade. The only time in my life I've ever gotten mad at Hank. I'd had this book report due and I'd spent about a week making a diorama of *Millions of Cats*, complete with a papier-mâché kitty. I'd left it on the stairway and when Hank came downstairs in the morning, he bumped it and it went crashing to the floor. The kitty broke into bits and the box caved in on one side.

I knew it was an accident. And probably even my fault. Not probably. It *was* my fault. I should never have left it on the stairs. But I screamed and screamed at Hank, blaming him for everything.

I looked at myself in the wavy mirror of the girls' bathroom. I knew what those boys this morning had been feeling. Sometimes, you just have to have someone to blame. Even if it's the wrong person.

But I'd grown up in Japantown. I knew better. Mrs. Harada was like an auntie to me. Betty and her family were church friends. They weren't responsible for Pearl Harbor.

Were they?

Bud walked me home but I hardly knew he was there. I was opening the front door when I heard him say, "Piper?" He stood at the bottom of the steps, holding my books out to me. I took them and started inside. He said my name again and then he said, "Hank's a tough guy. It would take more than a bunch of Jap planes to stop him." When he said *Jap*, it felt like a punch in the stomach.

"Don't say that word!" I snapped at him.

"I didn't mean anything by it." He looked so confused. "Everybody says it."

I was pretty sure I was going to start crying again and that was the last thing I wanted to do in front of Bud. "I'm just upset. I'll see you tomorrow, okay?"

The phone was ringing when I stepped inside the house. It was Pop saying he'd be home late. Really late. A bunch of men from the Japanese community had been arrested, mostly Issei, who were born in Japan, but even some Nisei, who were born here in America. Who were American. I asked if any were from our church. Pop sighed heavily into the phone.

"About half of them. Including Mr. Harada."

Mr. Harada? He was a regular Santa Claus. And

about as suspicious as a Bible salesman.

Pop said the FBI came to their house last night and took him away. They didn't even let him get his razor or toothbrush. Pop had spent all day trying to figure out where the men had been taken. He told me if any other parishioners called, I was to have them contact the church.

Margie had a late lab so I was all by myself. I couldn't stop listening to the radio. I had this feeling that if I keep it on long enough, I'd hear that Hank was okay. Maybe one of those announcers would come on and say, "We interrupt this program with an important message," and tell us that this Pearl Harbor stuff was all a hoax, like that *War of the Worlds* broadcast a few years ago.

When Margie got home, she came in and listened with me. We sat in front of the radio until the stations went off the air again but I never heard what I was listening for.

Tuesday, December 9, 1941

DeeDee —

Trixie called a little while ago and said she was sure I'd soon be wearing something new on my sweater set. She meant Bud's DeMolay pin, of course. She didn't even ask if we'd heard anything about Hank!

"My brother's at Pearl Harbor, Trixie," I told her. "We haven't heard from him. That's what I'm thinking about now, not going steady."

She said she was sorry and that of course she cared about Hank and I was to call her the minute we learned anything. We talked for a while longer. Or rather, she talked. About Debbie Sue's brand-new genuine pearl necklace and how the boy next to her in Civics has halitosis and that she and Eddy had argued at lunchtime over whether Humphrey Bogart or James Cagney was the better tough-guy movie star. As if any of that mattered.

My mind drifted during our one-sided conversation until I heard her say Betty Sato's name. Trixie was asking if I'd heard what happened to her at school.

I told her that I'd been there, seen it. I didn't tell her that I didn't say anything to those boys, or say anything to Betty. "It was awful," I said.

"But she *is* Japanese. And they bombed our troops."

I rubbed my tired eyes with my free hand. Trixie kept talking, saying that Debbie Sue's father was going to call the school board, to tell them they should expel the Japanese kids. For their own safety.

I felt like I used to when I was little and I'd done too many twirlies on the swings at school.

"Piper? Are you still there?" Trixie asked.

"Do you think her dad's right? Well, maybe we shouldn't stop with them. Maybe we should kick out the German kids." I was so angry, the words kept bubbling out. "The Italians, too."

Trixie was quiet for a second but when she spoke again, I could hear the hurt in her voice. "I'm your friend, remember?"

"I'm sorry, Trix." I took a deep breath. "It's just confusing. That's all."

"I know. It's okay."

But was it?

Wednesday, December 10, 1941

DeeDee —

We had our normal classes. Kids still goofed around in the halls. The cafeteria ladies still made meat loaf for lunch — after all, it was Wednesday.

But underneath all the normal activity slithered

a snake of mistrust. My classmates were looking at the Japanese kids in a different way. In homeroom, someone—I don't know who—left a note on Anky Arai's desk. Anky's the class clown and is always good for at least one joke during the period. Not today. He crumpled up the note and sat in stony silence. When the bell rang, he slammed the ball of crumpled paper in the wastepaper basket on his way out of class.

By the time lunch rolled around, my stomach was clenched as tight as a fist. I was so glad to slide onto the bench next to Trixie at our gang's table. It felt good to do something normal, something familiar. I picked at my meat loaf while Trixie told the table about the pop quiz her French teacher had sprung on them.

"Ooh, la, la," she said in her best French accent. "Mademoiselle Burke, how can you not know ze difference between *gauche* and *adroit* by now?" Even though I knew Trix felt bad about the quiz, she had us all laughing. Maybe we all laughed harder than we needed to. It felt that good to laugh at something.

The laughter stopped when Debbie Sue Wilkins slapped yesterday's *Seattle Times* on the table. "Did anyone see this interesting article?" she asked.

"Aw, save the current events for Civics," Eddy complained. I hunched down in my seat, hoping it wasn't the article I thought it was. No such luck.

Debbie Sue noisily flipped the paper open on the table and pointed to a headline: CHURCH MEN ASK FRIENDSHIP FOR JAPANESE HERE. "Listen to this," she said, and began to read aloud. "'These people are no more responsible for this war than we are,' said Pastor Emery Davis." Debbie Sue put down the paper and looked right at me. "That's your pop, right?"

She knew that it was. I didn't say anything. Neither did anyone else. Not even Bud.

Trixie slipped her hand through my arm. She tugged me away from the table. "Let's go, Piper," she said. "It smells funny here."

Debbie Sue made a big show of folding up the paper as Trixie and I got up. Debbie Sue had to get in one last shot. "It looks like some people are pretty quick to forget who it was that bombed Pearl Harbor."

Bud stood up, too. "Can it, Debbie Sue." He and Eddy left with me and Trixie. Having them next to me was the only thing that kept me able to put one foot in front of the other.

"You okay?" Bud asked.

I said sure, but how could I be? As much as I hated Debbie Sue Wilkins, there was something in what she said. We had no idea where Hank was, if he was okay or not, and Pop was out there giving interviews, defending the Japanese. Could he really be absolutely, positively sure none of them in Seattle were spies? There could always be one bad apple in the bunch.

"Piper, did you hear me?"

Bud was talking to me. "Sorry. What?"

"I said I'll see you later." He patted my arm. "Forget about Debbie Sue."

"It's not Debbie Sue," I said. Then my throat tightened up and I could feel tears at the backs of my eyes. I was not going to cry at school!

I went to get a drink of water. The drinking fountain was right next to a glass display case. I didn't have to look in it to know it held about a dozen pictures of Hank — on the baseball team, the basketball team, the football team. And I didn't have to look to know that in every single one of those pictures, he was standing next to someone like Tom Watanabe or Yosh Nakata or Ike Terada. Someone Japanese.

His friends. Our friends.

Bud walked me home but I wasn't good company. It was a pretty quiet walk. When we got to my house, I turned to go in. Bud stopped me. "Hank's tough, Piper. If anyone is going to make it, it'll be him."

I nodded and ran up the steps.

Later

I was in the kitchen, pouring some ginger ale to settle my stomach, and the phone rang again. Pop answered it.

He listened for a few minutes. Suddenly, he slapped his hand against the wall and swore. My father the minister swore! That made my stomach even queasier. He listened some more, hung up the receiver, and dialed Mrs. Harada. Whoever had been on the phone had found out where Mr. Harada was: in the Immigration Jail by the airport. Pop told her to put together a kit with a razor and toothbrush and other toiletries and he'd be by in half an hour to drive her there.

No amount of ginger ale can help my stomach now. How can Mr. Harada be in jail? What did he do? There are so many questions I wanted to ask, but Pop was out the door before I could ask them. Margie had the car keys jingling in her hand. She said, "You're too upset. I'll drive you." Pop never lets anyone else drive the Blue Box, but now he didn't say boo.

Sometimes I really don't get Pop. Ministers are supposed to preach sermons and baptize babies and marry people. It's one thing to help our friends, like Mr. and Mrs. Harada, but couldn't he do it in a way so other people wouldn't notice? The pastor at Trixie's church is a nice guy, a good pastor, and he isn't getting *his* name in the paper over all this fuss.

Pop had gotten phone calls and letters before, telling him to stick to his own kind. But that was before we were at war. What if the FBI didn't stop with Japanese? What if they arrested Pop?

I didn't know how to keep those bad thoughts out of my head so I wandered around, rearranging doilies on the backs of chairs, picking up magazines and putting them back down, straightening Pop's papers piled up all over the house. Then I found myself in Hank's room. When I was a pesky little kid, he never yelled at me to stay out of his room. And he never minded when I wandered in to borrow a Hardy Boys book from his collection.

You couldn't tell by walking in that Hank was even gone. The quilt Mrs. Harada made him was folded on the foot of the bed. The photo of him swimming in Lake Washington with Yosh and his other buddies sat atop the dresser. His letterman's jacket hung on a hook by his baseball trophies. I ran my hand down the sleeve, then put it on. The heavy wool still smelled like Hank, equal parts Aqua Velva and Black Jack gum. With that warm jacket wrapped around my shoulder, I felt like Hank was there, in the room, giving me a big-brother hug.

That must mean he's okay. It must.

Thursday, December 11, 1941

DeeDee —

I still can't believe what happened today. Mr. Tokita was walking home from his grocery store when these three guys came out of the alley and started calling him names. He kept walking but they chased after him and beat him up! Someone passing by found him on the sidewalk and drove him to the hospital. He's going to be okay but they have to keep him there for a day or two. I babysat while Pop took Mrs. Tokita to visit him. Her eyes were all puffy and red when they got back. She was upset and not just from seeing her husband. She told me that when Pop was driving her home, a group of boys came out of nowhere and started throwing rocks at the car. They called Pop a "Jap lover." One rock cracked the Blue Box's windshield.

Mrs. Tokita is worried but Pop says they're just kids and not to pay them any mind. Sometimes he makes me so mad. He thinks doing the Lord's work protects him. Well, what about all the apostles? They did the Lord's work and didn't exactly stay safe and sound. But there is no arguing with Pop.

Between worrying about him and worrying about Hank, I'm not getting any sleep.

I'm sure we'll hear something tomorrow.

Monday, December 15, 1941

DeeDee —

It was in the news this morning — everything they know about Pearl Harbor so far.

The attack took everyone by surprise. It'd been the last thing anyone expected on that quiet Sunday morning. There'd been some Christmas parties the night before and lots of the servicemen were sleeping late. One eyewitness — an Army guy who had a date to go roller-skating — looked up in the sky and saw a squadron moving in formation over the island. He thought it was some kind of drill, thought they were our planes. Until machine guns began blazing. He ran to his post, his pair of roller skates still around his neck.

Everyone seemed to be running somewhere — pilots ran to their parked planes at Hickam Air Force Base, sailors at Ford Island naval base ran to their battle stations, and civilians ran to get away from the bombs, dropping in deadly precision. One even landed right in front of the governor's mansion.

For three long hours, the Japanese attacked. Then, it was over. So many people died; they think maybe two thousand servicemen. And regular people died, too. The announcer said one of them was a two-year-old girl named Shirley Hirasaki. And there were still many, many people unaccounted for. Like Hank.

The entire U.S. Pacific fleet, over 130 ships, had been docked at Pearl Harbor. At least four of those ships are now on the bottom of Pearl Harbor — the *Utah*, the *Shaw*, the *Oklahoma*, and . . . I can't write the name of the other one.

There are survivors. Please, God, let Hank be one of them.

Tuesday, December 16, 1941

DeeDee —

I made a deal with God. If He keeps Hank safe, I will:

> Never wear lipstick or dungarees
> Give up Sky Bars for the rest of my life
> Go to church cheerfully every Sunday
> Never, ever again complain about being a
>   preacher's kid

Wednesday, December 17, 1941

DeeDee —

Ten days since the attack. I feel like we are a shadow family. Our bodies are moving around to all the places we're supposed to go — Margie to college, me to school, Pop to church — doing all the things we're supposed to do, saying the usual things like, "Yes, school was good today," "I got an A on that Chem lab," or "Please pass the salt." But our real family is in the shadows, frozen in time and hanging on to every scrap of hope, while we wait, wait, wait to hear about Hank.

Margie says be thankful that we haven't received

a telegram. The Wests got one a few days ago and today Sally and her mother changed the star on the service flag by their front door from blue to gold. Lots of families have these flags in their windows. A blue star on the red background means you have someone in the service. A gold star means that person was killed.

Danny West was only eighteen years old. Hank's age.

Please, God — no gold stars for us.

Thursday, December 18, 1941

DeeDee —

Miss Mahon called some Chinese students down to her office today. They showed up at school wearing buttons that said CHINA. After what happened to Mr. Tokita, I can see why they did it. Some people really can't tell the difference between Japanese, Chinese — even Filipino. Those kids wanted to make sure people knew they're from China, not Japan. But I saw Betty Sato when one of the Chinese kids walked by her, wearing that pin. She flinched, like she'd been hit. I don't think the Japanese kids need one more reminder of who dropped those bombs on Pearl Harbor.

I don't know what Miss Mahon said, but I can imagine. I didn't see anyone with those pins the rest of the day.

Friday, December 19, 1941

DeeDee —

Bud and I got an A on our project. Miss Wyatt said the interviews added a lot of "depth." I'm glad we're done. I didn't want to do any more of those man-in-the-hall interviews. I don't need to. I know how the war affects people. It makes you feel like you're on the world's tallest Ferris wheel ride and the safety bar is broken and you're stuck at the top with some crazy person who's swinging the car back and forth. It's having a constant stomachache and bad dreams and bad thoughts that you might never see your brother again.

That's how it feels.

Saturday, December 20, 1941

DeeDee —

Margie came home from her date with Stan, all red-eyed. Turns out she can cry, but only when she's really, really happy. See, she's happy about the new ring on her left hand! Stan's enlisted in the Army and they're going to get married before he leaves. I took pictures of them both, to put in a photo album I'm making to send to Hank when we hear from him. Because we *are* going to hear from him.

Stan's a good guy so I'm happy for Margie. But I'd like to find my brother before I lose my sister.

Is that too much to ask?

Sunday, December 21, 1941

DeeDee —

A stomachache wasn't a good enough excuse for Pop. He said I needed to go to church, to keep to our routines. And to be with our church family. I went because of my deal with God.

When I got there, Mrs. Harada came up and squeezed me in one of her Tabu-scented hugs. She said she was praying for Hank. I'd been so wrapped up in my worries about him, I'd hardly thought about poor Mr. Harada in jail, or even about Mrs. Harada. I was ashamed of myself. The Haradas have done so much for me. Mr. Harada taught me to ride a bike, and, when I was little, he always made sure he had butterscotch drops in his pocket for me. And Mrs. Harada, well, she's the closest thing to a mother I've ever had. The next time Margie takes supper over there, I am going to go along.

Today, Miss McCullough, a missionary who'd spent a lot of time in Japan, was playing the organ. She asked me to turn pages for her. During "A Mighty Fortress Is Our God," I looked out over the congregation. The newspapers talk about the "yellow menace," but the faces I saw around me weren't yellow. And they certainly weren't menaces. I mean, Mrs. Harada? The only way she'd be a danger is if you tried to help her in her kitchen. Our neighbor's yappy poodle is more dangerous.

I glanced to the far side of the church, to the pew where the Sato family usually sits. Mr. Sato sat at one end and Mrs. Sato at the other, with Betty and her big brother, Jim, and two little brothers, Mikey and Tommy, in between. Jim and Hank used to pal around a bit; he's a nice guy, but quiet. I know Pop thinks Betty practically walks on water, with her good grades and playing the piano, but I shouldn't hold that against her. We're probably not all that different, really. She wears her hair the way all the other junior high girls do — I bet she even sets it on pin curls, like me. And she dresses like practically every girl in America, in wool skirts and matching sweaters with a string of drugstore pearls. And even from the front of the church, I could see she wasn't wearing lipstick, either. Like me.

Pop says she's kind of shy. Maybe that's why we've never talked that much, gotten to know each other. I looked at her again and she caught me. She has a nice smile.

I made up my mind that I was going to go up to her after church. But Miss McCullough started talking to me about something and by the time I got away, the Satos were gone.

Next Sunday, for sure.

Monday, December 22, 1941

DeeDee —

Hank's alive!!!!!! Hank is okay! My heart's pounding so hard, I might explode. Can't write now.

Later

I bet this is what a prisoner feels like when he's let out of the hoosegow. Except instead of being free from being locked-up, I'm free from being worried and afraid! I feel so light and happy, it doesn't seem possible that my feet are touching our linoleum floor. We got the best-ever early Christmas present — a postcard from Hank. The Navy had all the sailors in Pearl Harbor send them to their families. Pop read it aloud, which didn't take long. Hank had only written four words, "Don't worry. I'm fine." Up in the left hand corner, he'd scribbled the date, December 9th — I don't know why it took so long to get to us but now I don't care. My brother is safe! That's all that matters. We all hugged and cried after Pop read the postcard. Even Stan.

Pop brought out some root beer and we toasted. "To Hank!" Pop said.

We clinked our glasses and said, "To Hank."

After our first sips, though, everybody got real quiet. Nobody said it out loud, but I think we were all wondering about the other two Musketeers. If their family had gotten this same kind of postcard.

Tuesday, December 23, 1941

DeeDee —

I caught Trixie before Language Arts to tell her our good news. She was chatting with Debbie Sue and some other girls but she broke right out of the circle when she saw me. She grabbed my arm.

"You heard something. I can tell," she said, then closed her eyes. "Please let it be good."

I told her and we ended up bawling right there in the hall. It was contagious — even girls who didn't know me or Hank were crying.

Debbie Sue cried the loudest but knowing her, that was for show.

Wednesday, December 24, 1941

DeeDee —

Christmas Eve services started early tonight so the Japanese families could get home before the curfew. In past years, it's been such a big deal preparing for Christmas — shopping, baking, and decorating the church. This year, we didn't even hang our stockings at home. It's funny how things you always thought you couldn't live without — like a Christmas tree or fruitcake — don't matter as much when something really important, like a war, happens. I mean, last year, I thought I would die if I didn't get that heathered green cardigan sweater and this year I don't care if there's one present under the tree with my name on it. I got my brother for a present and that's all I care about right now.

Right before the last hymn, all the lights in the church were turned off. The choir members handed out candles to everyone. They lit their own candles from the ones on the Advent wreath and then carried the light to someone in the congregation. As each candle was lit, the dark room flickered to life with soft, warm light. Miss McCullough played the first notes of "Silent Night" and the congregation began to sing together.

It was so beautiful, with the lights and the music, that I started to cry. The tears ran down my face for so many reasons — the biggest one was feeling joy and relief over Hank. But I was crying out of sadness, too.

I thought about what happened to Betty at school, and Mr. Tokita getting beat up, and Mr. Harada being in jail, and those boys throwing rocks at Pop's car, and wondered when we'd be able to sing *"all is calm, all is bright"* again and really mean it.

Thursday, December 25, 1941

DeeDee —

We got a telegram after all. I nearly threw up when I saw the delivery boy standing on our front porch, shivering in the rain. I tried to call for Pop, but only a squeak came out of my mouth. Margie and I held each other while Pop fished out a dime for a tip.

But it wasn't bad news! It was from Hank, telling us that John, one of the Musketeers, was in San Francisco. And he'd be in Seattle by the New Year, so could we please go visit him.

"Why does John get to come back and Hank doesn't? And what about Del?" I wanted to know. Pop looked at the telegram one more time before he answered. Only the injured sailors and soldiers were being shipped home. "So that must mean Del's all right, too?" I said, but Pop didn't say anything.

We didn't have a tree or presents and dinner was macaroni and cheese, but today was one of my best Christmases ever. I know there's a war going on, but I was so happy about Hank that nothing could dampen my holiday spirit. I felt like we were living Charles Dickens's *A Christmas Carol*, and I hobbled around pretending I was Tiny Tim, saying, "God bless us, everyone," in a terrible British accent. Pop and I made divinity fudge, and Stan came over and we all listened to Christmas carols on the radio and talked about what we'd do to make John feel welcome. We were almost as excited as if Hank were coming home. Almost.

Sunday, December 28, 1941

DeeDee —

Now the police are telling the Issei that they have to turn in their radios and cameras and stuff. If it weren't so scary, it might be funny. Imagine — Grandma Harada taking photos of top secret Army stuff! She's so frail, she'd probably fall over just trying to pick up the camera.

But they took the Haradas' camera, anyway. And their radio, too.

Tuesday, December 30, 1941

DeeDee —

Today's letter from Hank looked like one of those paper snowflakes I made in first grade. Pop said the censors have to cut out anything that might hurt the war effort. There was one part that I wished *had* been cut out. It was bad news. Only two of the Three Musketeers made it off the *Arizona*. Along with over one thousand other crewmen, Del had gone down with the ship.

I prayed extra hard for John. It would be horrible to lose your brother.

Wednesday, December 31, 1941

DeeDee —

The last night of the old year. A sad year. I'm praying that we win the war, and quickly.

I heard Debbie Sue Wilkins was throwing a New Year's Eve party. And that all the cool kids in seventh grade were invited.

Trixie and I made popcorn and fudge and played charades and planned never to invite Debbie Sue to any of our parties when we were rich and famous. We laughed ourselves silly and ate ourselves sick, all the while wondering if Bud and Eddy were at her party.

Once, Trixie got all sniffly. "Eddy's the only boy for me," she said. "What if Debbie Sue gets her hooks in him?"

"Let her have him!" I told her. "Boys. Who needs 'em? Besides, we'll always have each other, right, pal?"

That made Trixie laugh all over again. I laughed, too, extra loud to cover up the fact that I'd been worrying the same thing about Bud.

Thursday, January 1, 1942

DeeDee —

I've made some New Year's resolutions:

> I resolve to spend more time on my studies
>   and my photography.
> I resolve not to waste my time on boys.

Bud *was* at Debbie Sue's party. Not that I'm going to talk to him again when school starts. But if he *does* try to talk to me, I'm going to listen without saying anything and then when he's done, I'll say, "Good day, Mr. Greene," just like the leading ladies do in the movies.

That'll show him.

Sunday, January 4, 1942

DeeDee —

There is one more empty seat in the congregation now. Yesterday, the FBI went to the Satos' house. I overheard Mrs. Sato telling Pop about it after church. I found Betty down in the fellowship hall, getting juice and cookies for her little brothers.

I asked her if she was okay. She nodded yes, but bit her bottom lip. I think she was trying not to cry.

I grabbed us each an oatmeal molasses cookie and took her into the far corner of the hall. "Here," I said. "This is Mrs. Harada's special recipe. Guaranteed to fix anything."

She gave a weak smile, but just played with her cookie. "Nothing can fix this, Piper." She ducked her head down and sniffled.

"Do you want to talk about it?" I handed her a tissue from my pocket. First she shook her head no, then she blew her nose and started talking.

"They pounded on the door about eight o'clock last night. Dad was already in bed. Jim answered the door and there were these two men on the front porch. They said they were FBI and wanted to search the house. Jim called for Mom and she came out of the kitchen. By then the guys were already inside, picking up couch cushions, dumping books off the shelf onto the floor, shuffling through my piano music. They even came in my bedroom!" She blew her nose again. "They took my radio and Jim's binoculars. They even took Mikey and Tommy's Indian-head penny collection." She looked at me. "Why would they do that?"

I didn't answer. How could I?

"Mom started hollering at them that we're American citizens and they have no right to search our house without a warrant. That's when one of the guys pulled out a piece of paper and said that they did have a warrant. A warrant for Dad."

I felt like Betty and I were in a bad dream. This couldn't be happening.

She crumpled up the soggy, shredded tissue. I handed her another one. "You can't imagine what it's like to see the FBI take your dad away. We don't even know where they took him."

I patted her arm. "It'll be okay. Pop will find him."

Betty looked straight at me. "Your father may be able to find him. But it won't be okay. Nothing is okay." She stood up. "Thanks for the tissue. And for listening."

She tossed her uneaten cookie in the trash on her way out of the fellowship hall.

I did the same.

Monday, January 5, 1942

DeeDee —

I stopped at Wright's Drugstore after school to pick up a box of aspirin and some Vicks VapoRub for Pop. I was in line behind Jim Sato, Betty's big brother, but the clerk started to ring up my things first. I pointed out that Jim was there before me. The lady got all scrunch-faced and glowered at Jim. "But he's a J—" Before she could finish her sentence, Jim took off his baseball cap and swept it in front of him, bowing low like some grand gentleman, and said, "Ladies first, of course," in this fake English accent.

So I curtsied and said, "Oh, no, my good man. Age before beauty." We were both laughing. Jim started to bow again but the lady rolled her eyes and grabbed the market basket from his hands and rang up his purchases. When she rang me up, she didn't even say, "You're welcome," when I said, "Thank you." She pushed my sack with the aspirin and VapoRub in it at me and told me to get on home.

Jim held the door for me and tipped his hat again when we were outside. I always thought he was so quiet. Maybe it was because Hank and his other buddies were so loud and rowdy that I didn't have a chance to get to know him. He has awfully handsome eyes behind those glasses. And what he did in the drugstore was what Hank would've done, trying to lighten a tight situation with a joke. As we went our separate ways, he told me not to take any wooden nickels.

That's what Hank says, too. It must be a big brother thing.

Tuesday, January 6, 1942

DeeDee —

Bud cornered me after homeroom. "Where were you?" he asked.

"In class," I said, in my primmest voice.

He tapped me on the arm. "I don't mean just now, you nut. I meant on New Year's. I only went to Debbie Sue's party because she said you'd be there."

"What?" I looked into his green eyes. How could

they be telling anything but the truth? "I guess my invitation got lost."

"So I'm forgiven?" he asked.

"For what?" I said, pretending I hadn't been ignoring him since school had started up again.

"For everything. Anything!" He laughed. "Friends?"

How could I resist? "Friends."

"Then I'll meet you at your locker after school."

When he did, there was a note taped to my locker. Bud handed it to me and we read it together: "We don't need any Jap lovers here."

I asked him if I should show it to Miss Mahon and he said she wouldn't be able to do anything about it. He's right.

We both stood there a second, then he grabbed it out of my hand, crumpled it into a tight ball, and slammed it into the nearest garbage can. He said that's where that kind of stuff belonged. Only he didn't say stuff. "You're not letting this get to you, are you, Piper?" he asked me.

I looked into those dreamy green eyes and lied. "No, of course not. Sticks and stones, and all that."

How could it *not* get to me? The other day, the *Star* reported that Pop and some other ministers had been questioned by the FBI for their "work on behalf of the Japanese." And it wasn't even true. At least, not yet. It makes me so angry but Pop says we've got to turn the other cheek. That's easier to say than to do. Last night, some man called. He asked to talk to Pop and when I said he wasn't home, he asked, "Is this his daughter?" I was reaching for a pencil to take a message and said yes. The man's voice got angry. "What's it like to have a Jap lover for a father?" He said some other things, too, but I can't write them down. They're too ugly. I hung up the phone and didn't answer it when it rang again a few minutes later.

I'm running out of cheeks to turn.

Wednesday, January 7, 1942

DeeDee —

Betty Sato and I happened to go through the cafeteria line at the same time today and both reached for the same tapioca pudding for dessert. I could've easily asked her right then if she wanted to sit with us at our table. I mean, after all she was going through with her dad . . . I tried to make my mouth move. It was one thing to goof around with Jim at the drugstore. But here at school, in front of all of my friends . . . I lost my nerve. I went to sit with Trixie and the gang.

And Betty sat off by herself.

Like she has every day since Pearl Harbor.

Thursday, January 8, 1942
DeeDee —

When Bud walked me home today, he asked why I'd never taken his picture. I ran right inside and got my camera and then posed him in front of the rhododendron bush by the front porch. I made him take his trumpet out of its case and pretend he was blowing it. It took about twelve tries because he kept cracking up, then I'd crack up, but we both finally got a grip and I got the picture I wanted. I think. Through my viewfinder, with the low sun behind him, it looked like he was standing in a spotlight, playing taps.

Friday, January 9, 1942
DeeDee —

Another telegram from Hank. John arrives tomorrow. Pop, Margie, and I are going over to the hospital. Seeing John will be like getting ahold of a small piece of Hank. Not the real thing, but better than nothing.

Saturday, January 10, 1942

DeeDee —

Even though I'm not officially old enough to visit patients at the hospital, Pop said I was fourteen. Under his breath, he added, "Next August," so it wasn't a total lie.

It's a long walk from the front entrance of the hospital to the burn ward. That's where John is. The ward was full of sailors and soldiers from Pearl Harbor, some wrapped in so much gauze that they looked like mummies.

When we opened the door to the ward, all these horrible smells pounced on us like wild animals. Some of the smells I could identify — rubbing alcohol and cooked hamburger and bedpans. Some I had no idea what they were and I didn't want to know. It was better after Margie gave me a peppermint. That canceled out some of the odors.

This ward is packed. Bed after bed after bed filled with burn victims. It's because of all the fuel, pouring out of the sinking ships. It not only turned the harbor inky black — the men called it "black tears" — it caught on fire.

I forced myself not to cry when I met John. But it was hard not to. There are lots of things wrong with him, inside and out. He lost an arm, for one thing. His left ear is mostly gone and his neck looks like a washboard, covered with glistening rows of scarred skin. There's a big gash across his forehead and some other things that I couldn't see under the bandages and sheets.

The minute he found out who we were, his sad face lit up like we were his oldest friends. He shook Pop's hand and told him we should all be very proud of Hank.

"That day started out sunny. Blue sky. But by eight, the sky was so thick with Zeros. Too many to count, seemed like." He closed his eyes as if he was closing out the memory.

"You don't have to talk about it, son," Pop said.

"No. I want to. It helps." John reached for the cup of water on his nightstand, not even realizing he was reaching with the arm that wasn't there anymore. Margie quickly handed him the cup and he took a swallow. "It seemed like they'd just said, 'All hands, man your battle stations,' and we were hit.

Black greasy smoke was thick as tar. I could barely see where I was going, let alone breathe. Everything happened so fast. One minute, I was loading powder bags and the next I was in the harbor. I thought I'd died and gone to hell — sorry, sir." John looked over at Pop, who nodded at him to go on. "Instead of water, that harbor was full of fire. I figured if I wasn't already dead, I was gonna be soon. Then someone grabbed me. It was Hank. He held tight like I was some kind of glamour girl. I screamed at him to save himself but he would not let go." John blinked back some tears. So did I. "It seemed he dragged me along in that water for hours. But it couldn't have been. The first lifeboat we came to, Hank threw me in like he was firing a long throw in from center field. We tried to grab him, too, and pull him in, but he pushed off. He swam back toward the ship, grabbed another guy, and did the same thing all over again." John shook his head in disbelief. "I don't have any idea of how many men that crazy fool son of yours saved."

John said he didn't remember much about getting ashore. "All of a sudden, there was a nurse, sticking a needle in me. Morphine, for the pain. To make sure I didn't get another dose, she drew an *M* on my forehead with her lipstick." John grinned. "True Red, it was. I asked." He was hazy about what happened next. But as soon as he was able to travel, they put him on the ship to San Francisco, and then on the train to Seattle. "They're taking good care of me here," he said, "but nothing they do can get the taste of oil out of my mouth. I think I'm going to taste it until the day I die."

Pop got out his handkerchief and blew his nose. Even Margie was snuffling. I was teary, too, but I also felt like my heart would burst with pride. I hadn't wanted Hank to go to Pearl Harbor, but because he did, there were some sailors who didn't die.

I have the bravest brother in the world. But I want him home, quick, before he does something too heroic.

Tuesday, January 13, 1942
DeeDee —

This war stinks.

Later

All deals are off. I don't care if God strikes me dead for writing this, but I wish Hank had been hurt, like John.

It's not fair. It's not fair. He's a hero. He needs some rest. But we got a letter saying the Navy has put him on another ship, the USS *Enterprise*, which is heading to somewhere in the Pacific. Hank can't tell us any more than that. He made a joke, saying he was like our old cat, Admiral, with nine lives. So now, after Pearl Harbor, he has eight left. I didn't think it was a very good joke.

He ended the letter with a promise that he would take care of himself. That he would come home to us.

I bet you that's what Del told *his* family, too.

Wednesday, January 14, 1942

DeeDee —

Margie had homework and Pastor Thomson had picked Pop up for a meeting with a church committee, so I took the bus to go visit John. One of the stores downtown on Yesler had a big sign in the window that said NO JAPS.

I brought along the photo album I'm making for Hank. John had asked me to. I told him it wasn't finished but he said he didn't care. Teddy Baker, one of the other guys from the *Arizona*, wanted to look, too, so we went to the family waiting room. They parked their wheelchairs on either side of me. The three of us sitting in a row there made me think of the Three Musketeers. Even though John was smiling and joking, I could see pain deep in his brown eyes and wondered if he was thinking of them, too.

I started flipping through the pages. "Here's our church Christmas tree, and this is the squirrel that our neighbor leaves peanuts out for every day, and these are some pictures of our backyard."

"Slow down, Piper," John said. "You're going too fast." He turned back the page and pointed to one of the pictures. "Is that the tree house you and Hank built?"

I said yes, and then tried to tell them as much about each photo as I could. I cannot imagine, for the life of me, why John and Teddy wanted to look at Hank's album, but I noticed that by the time I reached the end, John's good hand wasn't shaking anymore and Teddy was smiling.

He looked at me and said, "'Course we don't have many pine trees or mountains in Kansas, but these here pictures made me feel like I took a trip home. Thanks, ma'am. Thanks a million."

John nodded. "This visit's been better than any medicine, Piper. You're a good egg."

I guess Pop's right — it is better to give than to receive.

Thursday, January 15, 1942

DeeDee —

President Roosevelt says we're all soldiers in this war. What he means is that we have to pitch in here at home. Right now, Pop's watching the miles he puts on the Blue Box because it's going to be hard to get new tires, what with the new tire rationing rules. Even though he was always kind of a lead foot — hard to believe of a preacher! — he's sticking to the Victory Speed Limit of thirty-five whenever he's on the road. The church is having a rubber drive on Saturday. Trixie and I went around the neighborhood, pulling her old red wagon, and collected three old garden hoses, four pairs of galoshes, two bathing caps, and one old tire.

Today's paper says these tire rations are only the first of the belt-tightening and predicts gas rationing within the next few months. Maybe food rationing, too.

I better stock up on Sky Bars!

Sunday, January 18, 1942

DeeDee —

A bunch of people from church went to the hospital with us today. Mrs. Harada and the Ladies' Circle brought Bibles and cookies for the men in the burn ward. Betty Sato came, too. She stood back in the corner, looking the way I looked on my first visit, I'm sure. At first the men didn't seem very happy to see the Ladies' Circle. I guess if I'd been at Pearl Harbor, I might have been kind of cold, too. Because they're Japanese and all. But Mrs. Harada is a steamroller of love and it wasn't long before she and the guys in the ward were joking around. She really took to John, treating him the same way she did Hank, all bossy like a mother hen. "You mind those doctors, John, so you get home soon-soon."

He said he would because he didn't want her coming after him. She was tougher than his Chief Petty Officer. That made her laugh.

When it was time to go, Mrs. Harada dabbed at her eyes and patted John's right hand. Betty walked out behind her mom, slipping something onto John's tray, between the coffee cup and dish of applesauce. I peeked at the tray as I walked out. It was a *tsuru* made of paper. A paper crane.

That gave me an idea.

Tuesday, January 20, 1942

DeeDee —

I got my courage up to call Betty and ask her about my idea. "I saw that origami crane you made for John," I said. "It was beautiful."

"They're for long life," she said.

"I know. And that's why I think we should make a whole bunch for the guys on the ward. To let them know we want them to have long lives. To give them hope."

"There are a lot of men," she said. "That would be a lot of work."

"We'll get some help." I was too excited by my idea to give up.

"I'll think about it," she said. And then she hung up.

Well, she didn't say yes . . . but she didn't say no!

Thursday, January 22, 1942

DeeDee —

Betty called me today. She didn't even say hello, but started out with, "What if we get all the Sunday school kids to help?" she said.

"So you'll do it?" I jumped up and down. "That's great."

"It'll take a lot of paper," she said. "Where are we going to get it?"

"Let me handle that." I had a pretty tidy nest egg saved up in my piggy bank.

But when I told Pop what we'd planned, he offered to buy all the paper we'd need. Then he hugged me and said, "A tree is known by its fruit."

Whatever that means.

Sunday, January 25, 1942

DeeDee —

All the Sunday school classes — even the four-year-olds — folded cranes to take to the hospital to cheer up the men. We made over two hundred! More than we hoped.

Tuesday, January 27, 1942

DeeDee —

So much for good deeds. The hospital wouldn't let us take the cranes around to the rooms. Wouldn't even let us leave them.

Nothing Japanese allowed. Some mucky-muck said it would be bad for the men's morale.

How could a token of goodwill be bad for anyone's morale? I tried to argue with the duty nurse but she just held up her hand. "Nothing I can do about it, kiddo," she said. "Now, get out of my hair. I've got work to do."

That box of two hundred cranes had been so easy to carry to the hospital. Afterward, I could barely manage to drag it onto the bus, to lug it home.

What had been a box full of hope was now a box of despair, heavy as lead.

Like my heart.

Friday, January 30, 1942

DeeDee —

Pop left the *Seattle Times* on the breakfast table when he went out this morning. It was folded open to a headline: ALIENS IN NORTHWEST MAY BE MOVED.

Even I knew what "aliens" meant: Issei. Like Grandma Harada or Mr. Tokita. They were born in Japan, not here. But moved where? How?

And what about their families? What would they do? Mrs. Tokita couldn't run the grocery store and take care of little Kenji by herself.

Just when you think things can't get worse, they do. It's all so unfair.

And scary.

Sunday, February 1, 1942

DeeDee —

Bud came over in the afternoon with news he'd heard. Planes from two American bird boats attacked Japanese bases on the Gilbert Islands.

One of the bird boats was the *Enterprise*.

I set up the game board while Bud counted out the Monopoly money. I was so distracted I even let Bud use the top hat, which is my good luck piece.

Bud rolled the dice again. "Ten spaces. Get out of jail free card!" he gloated as he added the card to his stack.

I picked up the dice and rolled. "Two." My Chance card said, "You crash your Studebaker into the mayor's house. Pay $200 fine."

As I counted out my money, Bud said, "Too late now! You didn't collect rent from me." He pointed to where his top hat sat on St. James. "That's the third time this game. Where's your head at?"

I shrugged. I didn't want to talk about where my head was at, which was far away, somewhere in the Pacific Ocean. It's hard to care about a game — even Monopoly — when your brother's ship could be involved in another battle. "Keep him safe" was the prayer I shot up to God, over and over again, like a toy arrow.

Margie asked Bud to stay for supper. She'd made wienies and beans but he acted like it was steak and had seconds. Pop looked impressed when Bud offered to help with the dishes, though he kept making excuses to come into the kitchen to check on us while we cleaned up.

Margie gave me the thumbs-up after Bud went home. "He's a keeper," she said.

Bud *is* nice, but I would trade all the boyfriends in the world to have my brother home.

Tuesday, February 3, 1942

DeeDee —

I stayed out of school today to babysit Mrs. Tokita's baby. Pop drove her and Mrs. Harada to the post office downtown. All "aliens" have to register, so they can get identification cards. When I handed the baby back to her after she got home, I noticed the ink smudge on Mrs. Tokita's finger.

Pop said they had to get fingerprinted, too.

Isn't that what they do to criminals?

Wednesday, February 4, 1942

DeeDee —

Pop's at another meeting and Margie's out with Stan. But I didn't mind being alone tonight.

I listened to Eddie Cantor — "It's time to smile!" — on the radio and added more pictures to Hank's welcome home album. The one of Stan and Margie after their engagement turned out good — they look so happy. And I got a cute one of the Tokitas' baby doing patty-cake last time I babysat. I even put in the one of Bud.

I didn't put in the picture I took of the Sunday school making paper cranes.

Thursday, February 5, 1942

DeeDee —

Pop picked at his meat loaf tonight so I knew something was up. I know he thinks I'm too young to understand what's going on, but Margie wasn't home for him to talk to so I dove in and asked what was bothering him.

He didn't answer right away but poked at his string beans. It turns out that Mr. Sato, Mr. Harada, and Mr. Tokita, along with some other men, maybe forty in all, were going to be sent to this place in Montana called Fort Missoula. Pop had spent all day trying to find out exactly when so he could make sure to be at the train station when they left. But so far, no one was telling him anything.

"Does Betty know about this yet?" I asked.

Pop said she did. I thought about that for a minute, about how scared she must be. I know I would be, if it were my father. "When you find out, would it be okay if I came along?"

"I think these families need all the support they

can get." Pop sighed. "Mrs. Tokita told me that baby Kenji said his first word yesterday. It was 'Da-Da.'"

There was spice cake with buttercream frosting for dessert but neither one of us had a taste for it. It didn't seem like there was anything sweet enough in the whole world to make this sour news go down any easier.

Friday, February 6, 1942
DeeDee —

In a funny turn of events, one of the newspaper reporters who has been hounding Pop and making him look bad in the paper was the one who let it slip that Mr. Harada and the others would be leaving from the King Street Train Station tomorrow morning.

You can bet me and Pop and my camera will be there.

Saturday, February 7, 1942
DeeDee —

It was raining pigs and chickens by the time we got to the train station. There were lots of people there but Pop and Pastor Thomson and I managed to find Mrs. Harada, Mrs. Tokita, and the Satos. I went over and stood right next to Betty. When the vans from the jail pulled up, all the Japanese men climbed out. Mr. Harada was last and he stumbled on the bottom step. Pop lunged forward to catch him, but the guards held him back. Mr. Harada caught himself on the man in front of him.

"Tozuko!" Mrs. Harada tried to make her way over to him. But the guards blocked her path. This really skinny guard said they'd had their chance to say good-bye at the jail. Mrs. Harada said please, just for one minute, but he pushed her aside.

Why would he treat her that way? She is one of the sweetest people in the whole wide world. Pop had moved toward the guard and was talking in low tones, trying to get them a few minutes together. But the guard wasn't having any of it. He and the other guards started pushing the men toward the train.

I wanted to yell at those guards. Ask them if they had families. Ask them if they'd ever heard of the Golden Rule. But I was pretty sure that would only make things worse. I had to do something, though, so I picked up my camera and started snapping. Mr. Sato walking backward so he could have one last look at his family. Mr. Harada dabbing at the rain—or was it tears?—on his kind face. It was so rainy and dark I didn't even know if any of these pictures would turn out. But I felt like I had to try. Had to help in some small way. If the families couldn't have proper good-byes, they could at least have photos of one another. The last photo I took that day was of Mrs. Tokita lifting up their baby, up as high as she could. She called, "Kenji! Kenji! Your son says good-bye," even after the men were jostled into train cars with their window shades pulled down tight.

When we got home, Pop asked if I was okay and I said I was probably catching a cold from standing around in the rain, *that's* why I was sniffling. He gave me a big hug and said he loved me.

What if Pop got taken away and I didn't have a chance to say good-bye?

Monday, February 9, 1942

DeeDee—

Trixie's going to the Valentine's Day Ball with Eddy.

Bud has had plenty of chances to ask me.

But he hasn't.

Friday, February 13, 1942

DeeDee —

Today's headline: TOTAL EVACUATION OF JAPS ON WEST COAST ADVOCATED.

The papers aren't talking about moving the Issei anymore; they're talking about moving all the Japanese, even those who are American citizens. The mayor of Los Angeles said he thinks they're more dangerous than the aliens! This is even scarier than when we had the blackouts after Pearl Harbor. Someone at school today said they heard the Japanese were all going to be rounded up and shot. Pop says that's ridiculous and not to listen to rumors.

People are acting crazy, too. Debbie Sue said her mom's organizing a committee to fire all the Japanese who are working in the schools. And Betty said her aunt and uncle who own an apartment house are nearly broke because their tenants won't pay rent to Japanese.

Pop says there's nothing for me to worry about but he's got dark circles under his eyes the size of dinner plates.

Saturday, February 14, 1942

DeeDee —

Who cares about a silly junior high dance? I hope Bud and Debbie Sue had a lovely evening. I know *I* did — because Stan and Margie got married! Sure, the ceremony took place in the living room, but that didn't stop it from being romantic. She wore her navy blue suit, with a gardenia corsage, and a new hat from Frederick and Nelson's. Stan looked dreamy in his freshly starched Army uniform. Pop did the service, of course, and it seemed like the sermon was extra long because he had so much to say about being a good husband and being a good wife so that when he finally got to the "You may now kiss the bride" part, Margie let out a whoop and threw her arms around Stan's neck. His face turned bright red and we all laughed.

Afterward, Mrs. Harada brought out her red velvet cake and paper cups of plum wine — I didn't get any. I took lots of pictures so Hank would feel like he'd been there with us. It wasn't like the society weddings they show in *Vogue* magazine, but it looked to me like Margie didn't mind one bit.

Monday, February 16, 1942

DeeDee —

Stan shipped out today. I heard Margie crying in the shower but when she came out, her face looked like it did on any other normal day. She did all her morning chores and even made a casserole for Mrs. Harada before she went to class. I guess you don't need to wear a uniform to be a hero.

Wednesday, February 18, 1942

DeeDee —

Margie got a job at Boeing! It means putting school on hold for a bit but she said if being a "Margie Mechanic" gets Stan and Hank home sooner, she's game. She showed me her new toolbox. So far it has exactly two tools in it. Her boss had kittens when he saw it but she told him she couldn't afford to buy more until the end of the month when she'll get paid, and that was that. She's something else! Everyone at work gets called by their last name, men *and* women. Since Margie's married, it's not "Davis," but "Robinson." The only person who doesn't get called by her last name is this one girl whose name is Norma Schanzenbach. The boss calls her "Schanzy."

Margie's a lucky duck to have such an exciting job and to really be helping with the war. Besides, she gets to wear slacks to work. It's regulation. She says she gets some fishy looks from people on the bus ride to work. One clerk at Woolworth's wouldn't even wait on her, said proper women wear dresses and hats and gloves. I don't care about being a proper woman! I wish I could be a Margie Mechanic, but I'm not old enough.

Thursday, February 19, 1942

DeeDee —

Pop told me he'd do up the supper dishes and now he's in the kitchen, clattering and clanking the pots and pans. He's really upset because President Roosevelt signed Executive Order 9066 to set up these military areas on the West Coast that certain people can't go in. I think this makes sense because you wouldn't want just anybody walking around top secret places during wartime, right? *Loose Lips Might Sink Ships*, isn't that what all the war posters say? Look at Margie — there are certain places she's not allowed to go in at the plant. It's common sense, right?

But Pop says it's not as simple as that. He says this order is going to be very bad for the American Japanese but I don't understand how.

Besides, things are already bad for them. There are signs all over town that say things like WE DON'T SERVE JAPS HERE, or TOJO, GO HOME. I don't know how they can get worse.

Saturday, February 21, 1942

DeeDee —

Betty and Jim were at the drugstore when I was picking up my pictures. Jim tipped his hat, which made me giggle remembering the last time we'd been there. Betty gave us both a look like we'd gone cuckoo. She asked me how Hank was doing, and I said fine even though we hadn't heard much.

I opened the envelope right there in the drugstore because I was so excited to see how my shots of Margie's wedding came out. There were a few duds, but not many. Maybe I *do* have an eye for photography, like Pop said. My favorite was the one of the new couple kissing. I decided I'd send Hank the more posed one, which showed Stan in his uniform beaming down at Margie. You could almost trace a heart around their heads. I was so caught up in studying the pictures that I didn't realize someone was leaning over my shoulder.

It was Bud.

I could feel my face turn redder than Hank's cherry red Ford truck. He was the last person I'd ever thought I'd run into. We hadn't even exchanged two words since the Valentine's Ball.

"It looks like a nice wedding," he said.

"Nicer than a dumb old dance," I said. And then I ran out of the drugstore, nearly knocking over some old man with a cane.

I wanted to curl up and die. Why did I have to say anything about the dance? Why couldn't I be a cool cucumber, like the female leads in all the movies are?

Why do I still have to have a crush on Bud?

Monday, February 23, 1942

DeeDee —

Miss Wyatt had been one of Margie's favorite teachers at Washington so I took in some pictures from the wedding to show her. She said Stan looked like a good man and I said he was. She asked which photographer took the photos and when I told her it was me, she was impressed. She thought they were professional! Said I have a real eye.

My pictures may have impressed her, but my latest essay didn't. I got a C.

Tuesday, February 24, 1942

DeeDee —

The *Enterprise* was in another raid. I didn't hear it from Bud this time — we haven't spoken since last Saturday — but read about it in the paper. It's funny — I've gone from being a kid who could barely finish the Sunday funnies to someone who reads the paper cover to cover every day. Especially if there's any mention of the Pacific. Which there is. A lot.

This latest fight was a raid on the Marshall Islands. They're kind of by New Guinea, but kind of not by anything — just tiny dots way out in the middle of the Pacific Ocean. I can't stand thinking of Hank so far away.

The good news is that it sounds like the Americans did okay in the fight. But I'd like to hear that from Hank himself.

I'd like to hear *anything* from Hank. It's been over a month since his last letter. That's not like him.

My fingernails are getting shorter each day.

Wednesday, February 25, 1942

DeeDee —

Betty Sato and I ended up waiting to cross 20th Street at the same time on the way to school this morning. This had happened before, but she was usually hurrying across to meet her Japanese girl-friends. This morning, though, she surprised me. "How are *you* doing?" she asked.

"Okay," I said. I mean, that's what you're supposed to say, right?

"I'm sure it's hard with Hank gone. And the fact that your father is who he is can't be easy, either."

No one else had ever said that to me. Everybody at church always said what a great guy Pop was, that he was taking a courageous stand. And Trixie and Bud kind of ignored anything Pop did. It felt kind of nice to have someone ask about what I was feeling. Especially someone whose own father was in a prison camp far away.

"I don't think it's easy for anybody right now." I fell into step beside her.

"Don't you know there's a war going on?" Betty was repeating a line we heard everywhere these days. We both laughed.

And that laugh felt so good! I asked her if she'd heard the latest episode of *The Shadow*, and we started talking about what might happen next—would the bad guys discover that Lamont Cranston was really the Shadow? She agreed with me that Sky Bars were a bit of heaven on earth. "How can any candy bar that's four in one not be the best, for Pete's sake," she said. It turns out her favorites are the peanut and vanilla sections and mine are the fudge and caramel. "It'll be easy for us to share one, then," I told her. "We'll each always get our favorite parts!" And we both agreed with each other that our parents were hopelessly outdated about makeup; her mom wouldn't let her wear any to school, either.

We talked about our dreams—she promised to buy any magazine with my photographs in it and

I promised to go listen to her play the piano when she made it to Carnegie Hall.

It was the shortest walk to school I'd ever had; we were at the front steps before I knew it. I wondered why we'd never done this before. It seemed like we had lots to talk about, lots in common.

The only thing we didn't talk about was that other day on the steps.

Saturday, February 28, 1942

DeeDee —

Trixie called and asked me to go to the show. She said it would help me take my mind off Hank and everything. I couldn't help but think of the last time we went to the movies together, with Bud and Eddy. With my luck, Bud would be there today. With Debbie Sue. Sigh. But Trixie's my best pal and I knew she was hoping to see Eddy so I said I'd go.

After my chores and before the movies, I took some pictures for Hank. The cherry trees in the churchyard were bursting with buds and they reminded me of Margie all frothy in pale green tulle for the Senior Dance two years ago. Mrs. Lee was sweeping the stoop of her little market, where

Hank and I always bought penny candy. He loves Neccos but not the brown ones, so he always gives those to me. I don't like them, either, really. I only eat them for Hank. I got a couple of pictures of Mrs. Lee. I have a good feeling about the one where she's framed in the doorway. I hope that one turns out. I finished off the roll with some snaps of Garfield High School, Hank's alma mater.

You won't believe who I met on the way to the theater. Here's a clue: His initials are B.G. And he was by himself. No Debbie Sue in sight. I tried to pretend I didn't see him but he called out my name. I couldn't be outright rude, could I?

It turns out his mom and Debbie Sue's mom play in the same bridge club and it was their idea he and Debbie Sue go to the dance together. I know it sounds like a phony excuse but I believed him. Those green eyes were so sincere. He ended up walking me all the way to the theater, before he headed off to do his paper route.

I wish I'd had my camera with me to capture the look on Trixie's face when I showed up with Bud!

Sunday, March 1, 1942

DeeDee —

It was John's birthday today. He's 22. We took him a birthday cake. It was my idea to put four candles on it, two for him and two for Del. When we got there, I was afraid that was a bad idea but he said he was glad I did it. He wants to remember Del. And he was glad that we remembered him, too.

I took a picture of him blowing out the candles. "What did you wish for?" Margie asked him. He winked and said he couldn't tell her that or it wouldn't come true. That made us all laugh.

After that, I gave him the present I'd brought.

"A dictionary?" Margie said when he opened it.

"It's just what I wanted," John said. "Not much to do in here but read and there are a passel of words in these books that I never heard back home."

He asked the nurse for a pen and had me write an inscription inside. I wrote, "For Professor John Anderson on his birthday. March 1, 1942. With love, Piper Davis."

When I handed it back to him, he smiled. "I like the sound of that. Professor Anderson."

His burns are healing right up. And you'd hardly know he only has one arm; he can do about everything now. He ate three pieces of cake while I read him the Sunday funnies.

The doctor is pleased with how he's doing and said they can start thinking about sending him home. Pop said that we should be happy for John. Of course he wants to go home.

But having him here makes me feel closer to Hank. And I don't want to let go of that.

Monday, March 2, 1942

DeeDee —

It's a good thing I was sitting on the porch steps; otherwise I would've fallen over in a dead faint when Bud asked me to be his girl. He gave me his DeMolay pin. My hands were so shaky I couldn't get the clasp at first. I got my compact out of my pocketbook and admired myself in the mirror. "It looks swell on you," Bud said.

I touched it lightly, pinned right over my heart. "I won't be able to wear it, you know. Pop would have kittens if he knew."

Bud reached over and squeezed my hand. "We'll know and that's all that matters."

And guess what else? Now I'll never be able to say that I'm "Sweet Sixteen and Never Been Kissed."

Wednesday, March 4, 1942

DeeDee —

Margie found Bud's pin when she was sorting clothes to do laundry. It had gotten tangled in one of my sweaters. She said she wouldn't tell Pop; that was my job. But she did suggest I invite Bud to dinner again, let Pop get to know him better, before I break the news.

Friday, March 6, 1942

DeeDee —

Bud came to dinner tonight. He even asked for seconds on Margie's meat loaf. I was so nervous, I couldn't eat anything. I was terrified that Bud might let something slip about us going together. Or that somehow, Pop would be able to figure it out. So far, so good.

After dessert, we all played Monopoly and promptly at nine o'clock, Pop said that it had been a pleasant evening and handed Bud his jacket. That's my pop.

Bud got a devilish look in those green eyes of his and pulled me out the door with him when he stepped out. He spun me around and gave me a quick kiss — all before I even knew what was happening.

Margie raised her eyebrows when I came back in, all windblown and breathless, but I don't think Pop suspected a thing. He was too engrossed in his newspaper.

Monday, March 9, 1942

DeeDee —

Another assignment for Miss Wyatt. This one's a biography. As I was leaving class, she called me to her desk and suggested I choose Margaret Bourke-White, the famous photographer, as a subject. She'd taken the first cover shot for *Life* magazine.

I didn't really know about her but she sounded interesting. More interesting than Admiral Halsey, the person Bud chose.

I'm going to go to the library at lunch tomorrow to see what I can learn about her.

Thursday, March 12, 1942

DeeDee —

Bud said if I tell him one more "interesting fact" about Margaret Bourke-White, he may take back his pin. He's kidding. I think.

But she is pretty amazing. Did you know she was the first Western photographer, male or female, allowed in the Soviet Union in the 1920s? And Henry Luce hired her to be one of the very first photographers for *Life* magazine. A woman!

She didn't start out wanting to be a photographer. She wanted to be a (shudder) herpetologist — someone who studies snakes. It wasn't that she loved snakes so much, it was because she wanted to go on jungle safaris and do things women had never done before. She is as brave as Superman — without the superpowers. So maybe that makes her even braver. I don't know if I could do the things she has done but it'd be something, wouldn't it? Can you picture plain old me flying off to Paris or Russia or Timbuktu, taking photographs that will end up in magazines that will end up in every house in America? After reading Margaret Bourke-White's story, I'm thinking, why not? If she can do it, why can't I? Trixie says when she's a famous movie star, I'll be the only photographer she'll allow to take her picture.

On Saturday, I'm going to the public library to see if they have any books of MBW's photographs.

Friday, March 13, 1942

DeeDee —

This is a lucky Friday the thirteenth — a letter from Hank. He says he's getting fat from all the "gee-dunks" he's eating — that's what they call ice cream in a cup on his ship. He also said they had a lively dance party a few weeks before. That confused me for a bit — a dance on a ship?! But then I realized he was talking about some kind of action. I wrote him right back: "Be careful! I want you home with all eight of the lives you have left."

Saturday, March 14, 1942

DeeDee —

Trixie could not believe I'd rather go to the library than to the show. Bud says I care more about Margaret Bourke-White than I do about him.

I can't help it! She's so interesting. I mean, how many people would climb up to the tops of skyscrapers to take pictures? She got into photography when she was a kid, too. About my age.

Maybe I *could* be a photographer for *Life* magazine, like Bud said.

Sunday, March 15, 1942

DeeDee —

Mrs. Tokita was sick today so it looked like I'd be on my own with the four-year-old Sunday school class. But she had called over to the Satos' and both Jim and Betty showed up to help.

There were only ten of the little guys but it seemed like a hundred. Two kids were fighting over a fire truck, one little girl was trying to give her friend a bang trim with the safety scissors, and another little girl sat in the corner, crying for her mama.

"Okay." Jim bounced to the center of the room. "Everybody look at me. Do you know how to play Simon Says?" Pretty soon, he had all ten kids laughing and following along, pretending they were elephants or hopping on one foot or sticking out their tongues.

While he had them distracted, Betty and I organized the arts and crafts. We found some white paper, cotton balls, and paste.

"We can make lambs," Betty said.

"Great idea!"

"Simon Says—time for crafts!" Ready or not, Jim led the kids over to the table. One little boy ate most of the paste before we realized it, but there was enough left over to do the craft. There were more cotton balls stuck to us and to the kids than to the paper, but the parents didn't seem to mind. They *ooh*ed and *aah*ed over what their kids made when they came for them after church. Jim, Betty, and I couldn't stop laughing as we cleaned up the classroom.

I don't think those little kids have ever had so much fun at Sunday school in their lives. And I don't think I've ever been so bushed!

Tuesday, March 17, 1942

DeeDee —

You'll never guess what my sister did! She sent that picture of Mrs. Lee in to the *Seattle Times* for a photography contest and it won. First prize! One of the judges is a professional photographer and he said the picture had "artful composition as well as heart."

There was a cash prize, too — $15. Pop said I had to save 10 percent of it and give 10 percent of it to the church, but that the rest was all mine.

I went out and bought more film!

And another tube of Tangee lipstick, which is hidden safely in my underwear drawer.

Wednesday, March 18, 1942

DeeDee —

Pop is pacing and fussing around like a caged cat. The papers are full of the news about President Roosevelt signing Executive Order 9102, "By virtue of the authority vested in me . . . it is ordered as follows . . ." The "as follows" part was hard to follow. But we went over it in Civics today. This order is about setting up the War Relocation Authority.

They're going to be the people responsible for moving people out of military zones, if that happens. What I don't understand is that, even if you read the whole thing—which I had to for Civics!—you don't see any mention of who the people are "whose removal is necessary in the interests of national security." Nowhere in the order does it say anything about Japanese people being relocated, but when I told Pop that, he said it was there, between the lines.

He's so upset. I even heard him on the phone with our state senator and congressman!

We took a vote in Civics class. Most of the kids think that what the president is doing is necessary to keep the country safe. Bud thinks so, too.

I didn't raise my hand either way. I sure don't want Japan to drop bombs on Seattle, but I don't want any more of my Japanese friends to be taken away.

Monday, March 23, 1942

DeeDee —

It's really happening. General DeWitt has ordered all "alien and non-alien persons of Japanese ancestry" to leave Bainbridge Island, just across the sound. I know that alien means the Issei, who were born in Japan. But what does "non-alien" mean? Someone who wasn't born somewhere else, right? So that would mean someone born here, in America.

An American citizen.

I don't believe President Roosevelt intended it to turn out this way.

Tuesday, March 24, 1942

DeeDee —

Trixie's dad says the sooner the better, but I don't understand the rush to move the Japanese. It's not like there's been any espionage or sabotage or anything like that since Pearl Harbor. Sure, there have been battles, but they've been in the Pacific Ocean, not on the Pacific Coast.

The people on Bainbridge have to be off the island by next Monday. That gives them only a week to figure out what to do with their cars, their houses, their farms. All in one week. When it's time to leave, they can only take what they can carry.

What would I take, if it were me? What would I choose?

How would I choose?

Monday, March 30, 1942

DeeDee —

They were taken away in trucks today. Over two hundred Japanese, mostly strawberry farmers and mill workers, Pop says, boarded the ferry *Kehloken* at the Bainbridge Island dock. High school kids skipped school to see them off; lots of neighbors came down, too. Pop said everybody — no matter their race — was crying. After crossing Eagle Harbor, the Japanese landed in Seattle, for a ride by bus or truck south to Puyallup. The fairgrounds there have been converted into some kind of camp where they're staying for now. Camp Harmony, it's called.

Pop and a couple of other ministers are going to visit them tomorrow.

Wednesday, April 1, 1942

DeeDee —

Someone with a bad sense of humor named Camp Harmony. There are families living in horse stalls — that still smell of horses! They had to stuff mattresses with straw to have something to sleep on.

After he got home, Pop went into his den and kept the door closed for a long, long time.

Sunday, April 5, 1942 — Easter

DeeDee —

Like always on Easter, the little girls were dressed up in their new bonnets and patent leather Mary Janes rubbed with Vaseline so they'd be extra shiny, and the little boys still ran around with their pockets stuffed with jelly beans, but I think they were the only ones who were truly joyful today.

Our little congregation generally makes a joyful noise unto the Lord, especially on Easter. But I think we were all still in shock about what happened on Bainbridge Island. I was sitting next to Mrs. Harada, and even she was kind of mouthing the hymns.

The few people who stayed around after church gathered in small groups, talking in low, worried voices.

I didn't see Betty or any of her family. I don't blame them. It'd be hard to feel like praising the Lord when your father's in jail.

Monday, April 6, 1942

DeeDee —

John called around suppertime. He's been cleared to leave the hospital! Cleared to go home! Part of me was as excited as he was. He misses his family and it's only natural he'd want to be back with them. But part of me was sad. Having John nearby helped Hank feel closer.

His train leaves on Friday, while I'm at school, so Pop's taking me over Thursday night to say goodbye.

Wednesday, April 8, 1942

DeeDee —

Mr. Afton showed slides of his trip to Washington, D.C., today in History and I fell sound asleep. The slides *were* boring, but I didn't get much sleep last night. Trixie poked me with a pencil to wake me up when the lights went back on. She's a pal.

The reason I didn't get much sleep is that right after Pop left for another one of his meetings, we got one of those phone calls. Once I heard the man's voice say, "You Jap lovers," I hung right up. Margie was working at the plant so I was alone. I double-checked all the doors, but still couldn't go to sleep. Finally, about 2 A.M., I went into Hank's room and crawled under the quilt.

Thursday, April 9, 1942

DeeDee —

I promised myself I wouldn't blubber, but I did. Saying good-bye to John was even harder than I thought it'd be. He promised to write, and I did, too.

I don't know where he got it, but he gave me a brand-new, blank photo album. He said it was for me to keep an album of my very own, not to give away to someone else. That way I'd have a nice collection to show *Life* when I was ready. What a dreamer! It is a beautiful album, though. The cover is edged with gold and the pages are heavy black paper. On the inside front cover, he wrote: "To Piper, Keep that shutter clicking. Your pal, John."

I felt as proud as Margaret Bourke-White must've when she got her first assignment. Now, I have to make sure I take pictures that are good enough for this album.

Friday, April 17, 1942

DeeDee —

I turned in my Margaret Bourke-White biography. At the last minute, I decided to include some of my own photos. Showing what I learned from her.

I told Miss Wyatt what I'd done, and she smiled and said she couldn't wait to read my report. That was a first for me! I don't think a teacher's ever been excited to read one of my assignments before.

When the bell rang to dismiss us, I noticed that Miss Wyatt slipped my report on top of the pile. That was better than getting an A! I was feeling so good that I was even pleasant to Debbie Sue Wilkins at lunch.

Saturday, April 18, 1942

DeeDee —

Margie's been moping around because she hasn't heard from Stan in a while. So Pop and I decided to go to Higo, the Japanese five-and-ten-cent store, to get some of those special rice candies she loves. We thought that might give her a lift.

When we drove up, we could see a big chain looped through the front door handles, fastened with a padlock as big as my math book. I peered in through the front window. Some paper fans, a couple of ladies' hats, and a box of Sweetheart straws lay scattered on the counter. A wooden tricycle painted to look like a duck was tipped on its side on the floor. Otherwise the store was bare. Pop and I drove around the rest of Japantown. Every store on Jackson Street was boarded up. Posters advertising The Amazing Dante Magic Show were pasted all along the boards. A rumpled brown paper sack skittered along the sidewalk. The entry to the Maynard Hotel was strewn with garbage. Mrs. Ito would've died if she'd seen it. She kept the front of that hotel spic-and-span.

It was like we were driving through a ghost town. All those businesses, all those people, gone.

My insides felt as empty as Higo's shelves.

Tuesday, April 21, 1942

DeeDee —

Betty and I were walking home from school, sharing a Sky Bar, when we saw a soldier posting a flyer on a telephone pole. When he finished and drove away, we hurried over to see what it said.

It was a notice, signed by Lieutenant General DeWitt. INSTRUCTIONS TO ALL PERSONS OF JAPANESE ANCESTRY LIVING IN THE FOLLOWING AREA. In small print, the area was described in detail. Basically, it was everything south of Yesler Way. All of *Nihonmachi*, Japantown.

Betty's hand dropped to her side. The rest of the Sky Bar fell to the ground. "Now it's us," she said in a voice flattened by disbelief and pain. She started running so fast, I couldn't catch her, even though I tried. I don't think she wanted me to, anyway. After a couple of blocks, I stood there, not sure what to do.

I ran back to read the rest of notice. It was in English, all right, but it could've been Greek. I recognized the words but they didn't add up. Didn't make sense.

All of our neighbors had to leave.

They had until noon, Friday, May 1, 1942.

By order of Lieutenant General DeWitt.

I tore the notice off the telephone pole and ran home, too. I had to show Pop. He would know what to do.

Saturday, April 25, 1942

DeeDee —

Bud and I had our first fight. He says our country should do everything possible to protect against spies and saboteurs. It's hard to disagree with that but what gets me mixed up is that I know that people like Mrs. Harada and Mrs. Tokita are not spies. They just happened to be born in Japan. And what about Betty and Jim? They were born here, just like me and Bud.

Bud says it doesn't matter. And besides, real Americans should be proud to do *anything* to help the war effort. "My dad tore up our whole front yard to put in a Victory garden," he said. "And that was like his baby."

Giving up a patch of grass is nowhere near the same thing as being sent to a relocation camp, leaving your own home. I tried to explain that to Bud but he wouldn't listen. "They're Japanese," he said. "Our enemies."

I stopped on the sidewalk and stared at him. "Mrs. Harada is not anybody's enemy." I could hardly talk straight. Mad feelings shot around inside me like marbles.

"Come on, Piper. Don't be unreasonable." Bud tried to take my hand but I jerked it away.

We walked home the whole rest of the way without saying another word.

Sunday, April 26, 1942

DeeDee —

A few years ago, the Nazis started making the Jews wear yellow stars whenever they went out. I'd never really thought about what it meant until today.

All of our friends from church have been issued tags. The government won't even use their names, just a number. They have to wear them when they leave on Friday for the assembly center.

The Satos are family number 10715. We found out when we visited them after church. Their five tags sat, tangled together, on the kitchen table. Everyone ignored them like they were a plate of cold, leftover fried liver. Tried to pretend they weren't there. Tried to pretend they didn't mean leaving. And worse.

I had my camera along because I was taking as many pictures as I could of the people from church in front of their houses. So they'd have a bit of home to take with them. Betty said I should take a picture of the tags, too. I wanted to make something nice, keepsakes. Those tags may only be made of cream-colored cardboard but they were ugly, like a barbed wire fence between neighbors. They stood for something ugly, too. But then Betty said, "Margaret Bourke-White would do it." And I realized that if I wanted to be a real photographer, I was going to have to take pictures I didn't want to. Take them because they were important for others to see. Like those photos Margaret Bourke-White took after that big flood in Kentucky a few years back. Those pictures helped the people who weren't in the floods understand what it was like. And understanding was sure something we could use right now.

Monday, April 27, 1942

DeeDee —

I went to the church straight after school to help Pop. We're marking the gym floor in the basement off in squares. Because the Japanese can only take what they can carry, people are already starting to bring their belongings to store here, even people who don't go to our church. I took pictures to send to Hank, but also to help us remember which containers were where.

By suppertime, half the squares were filled with cardboard boxes and old suitcases. It looks like we're having a church jumble sale.

If only that were the case.

Wednesday, April 29, 1942

DeeDee —

I met up with Betty again on the way to school. It looked like she'd been crying. I asked her if she was okay. Had she heard something from her dad? After about two blocks, she finally told me what was wrong. It's their piano. She's cleaned the white keys with milk every week since she was five. It's in perfect condition. But it's too big to take with them. Last night, her mom sold it to some lady who bought it for her granddaughter. Sold it for $25. That beautiful piano. There was a rock on the sidewalk by Betty's foot and she kicked it, really hard. It clattered into the gutter. "Twenty-five crummy dollars," she said.

She's right. It's crummy. So many things are

crummy. Betty shoved her hands in her pockets and we walked the rest of the way to school, our steps heavy and dull as a flat, low note on a piano.

Friday, May 1, 1942

DeeDee —

I have the wet hair and coat to prove it was real, but today seems like a bad dream. It rained from the minute we picked up Mrs. Harada until the last of the Japanese were loaded onto the buses. Pop and I got soaked, trying to fit in all of our good-byes.

Betty was dry-eyed when I caught up with her. "Mom keeps saying, '*Shikata ga nai*.' It cannot be helped." She shrugged. Maybe the evacuation couldn't be helped, but that didn't mean *I* couldn't cry about it. Betty is like Margie — tougher than I ever could be.

There were some rough-looking men hanging around the pick-up point. One big guy with a scraggly beard and a belly that bulged over his belt stood, arms crossed, glaring as people walked by them to the trucks and buses. He started shouting, "Get outta here, you Japs." Only he didn't just say "you Japs."

When it was Mrs. Harada's turn to get on the bus, she hugged me so hard, I could hardly breathe.

But I didn't want her to let go. I breathed in her lemony smell, remembering all the times I had smelled it while she read me stories and pushed me on the swings at the park. "Be a good girl," she told me.

"Pop's getting us passes. We'll come see you as soon as we can." I gave her one last hug, only letting go when a soldier pried us apart. Right before she stepped onto the bus, a photographer called out to her. "I'm going to take your picture. Let's have a smile." She smiled that warm, kind smile of hers, the flashbulb went off, and she was on the bus and out of sight.

The next day, her photo made the front page of the paper. The caption read: JAPS HAPPY TO GO.

I tore it up and threw it in the garbage.

Tuesday, May 5, 1942

DeeDee —

Two letters today. One from John, writing to let us know he'd arrived home safe and sound and that his mother was single-handedly trying to turn him into the fattest ex-sailor on the planet.

The other was from Hank. The censor had gone to town on this one and it was marked up pretty good. He said they'd seen lots of birds, especially red-breasted jays, which threw Pop for a loop. He didn't think jays could fly way out over the Pacific, which is where we were pretty sure Hank's ship was. Then it dawned on me: Zeros have big red balls painted on their wings and sides—"red breasts." Hank was telling us they'd seen some Japanese planes.

I was proud of myself for puzzling that out when Pop couldn't, but it's one message I could've done without.

Friday, May 8, 1942

DeeDee —

There are posters up all over the place that say EVERY CITIZEN'S A SOLDIER. What they mean is that we've all got to pitch in. There are rubber drives and scrap metal drives—Pop donated the front bumper from the Blue Box—and newspaper drives. Lots of the older girls are "Knitting for Victory," knitting socks and hats and even stretch bandages. Margie knits on her way to and from work, but says she is sick to death of using olive drab yarn. And everyone with even the smallest backyard is planting some kind of Victory garden, growing vegetables to be patriotic.

Pitching in means giving up, too, so the soldiers have plenty. Now sugar's being rationed. Pop's got to go to the school on Monday to get our sugar ration book. Trixie's mom picked their family's up yesterday and said it didn't do her much good. Sure, she had the coupon but none of the nearby groceries had sugar to sell.

Asking people to use less gasoline didn't work out very well, so now that's being rationed, too. Pop got a red "C" sticker for the Blue Box because he's a minister. Trixie said her dad had a conniption fit when he couldn't talk his way out of one of the green "A" stickers. That means he can only get four gallons of gas a week. Pop's sticker lets him get eight gallons but he's still scratching his head to figure out ways to make it go farther. He's already put a lot of miles on the Blue Box going back and forth to Puyallup.

An ad in the *Seattle Times* showed a housewife with a ration book, saying, "I'm in this fight, too." I guess we are *all* in the fight, now.

Saturday, May 9, 1942

DeeDee —

This is the Satos' new address: Area A — Section 4 — Apartment 101, Camp Harmony, Puyallup, Wash. Pop went to see them yesterday and brought me a letter from Betty. She wrote that Jim named their room "Knot Inn," because there are so many knot-holes in the boards. They sleep on mattresses stuffed with hay, which has made Mikey's hay fever act up. Between his sneezing all night, the lumpy, hard bed, and what she calls the "stranger noises," Betty isn't sleeping much. There are lines for everything, from the bathrooms and showers to the mess halls. The camp food is awful — lots of Vienna sausages and sauerkraut — so they feasted on the grapes Pop took.

He's going to take me with him next weekend. I'm spending my whole allowance on Sky Bars for Betty.

Sunday, May 10, 1942

DeeDee —

When I got up, Pop was in his "preaching" suit and tie. I looked over at Margie, who raised her eyebrows. After breakfast, Pop said that we didn't have to come if we didn't want to. "Come where?" I asked. When he turned his sad brown eyes on me, I knew what he meant: church.

Before I could say anything, Margie said of course we were coming with. Then she gave me a look that I knew meant business. We were both in our church clothes and ready to go at the usual time. As we were heading for the car, Pop asked me to grab my camera, so I did. Margie chattered the whole way but I didn't know what to say.

Like he has a million times before, Pop unlocked the door to the church. It's practically my second home, but it felt so strange. Mrs. Harada was usually right there, waiting for Pop, ready to go in and fix the altar flowers or set up the coffee for Fellowship Hour after church.

Pop got up behind the pulpit, like there were people there. Like church was really happening. Margie waved me into a pew and we sat there while Pop looked out over the "congregation."

I kept my coat on; Pop hadn't turned the switch for the heat. The buttons on my coat sleeve clunked loudly against the wooden pew. There weren't any other noises to cover up the sound. The sanctuary had always felt cozy and warm to me, filled with familiar faces. Sitting there on the pew, I felt like one of those blown eggs Mrs. Harada used to decorate for Easter, all hollowed out and easy to crack.

I needed to do something so I took some photos of Pop. I didn't think he noticed.

But he must've heard the shutter click because he asked me to come up and stand next to him. "Take a picture looking out there," he said. "Not that I'll ever forget this day. But it's important to remember it. That we all remember it."

I took the photo. Then he said the benediction, like he does at the end of every service.

On the drive home, it sunk in: With everyone in Camp Harmony, Pop doesn't have a church. And nobody knows when they'll be back.

I wonder what he's going to do.

Friday, May 15, 1942
DeeDee —

The headline in the *Seattle Times* today: LAST OF COUNTY JAPS GOING SOON.

I hate that word. It even sounds awful.

The newspaper didn't get it quite right, anyway. Maybe there's a few Japanese families somewhere in the county, but not around here. Japantown is as still as a cemetery. Our church is lonelier than the birdhouse in our backyard after the last chickadee has fledged. And all the empty houses in our neighborhood stare glumly at me as I walk to school.

My classmates carry on as if everything is normal, as if a quarter of our student population wasn't missing. We still have pep assemblies for the baseball team. The drama club is still going to put on *As You Like It*. The ASB is still selling tickets for the eighth-grade graduation ball.

I can't look at the posters without thinking of all the eighth graders who won't be going to the dance. Without thinking about Betty, who had already started making her dress and who won't even be here for the graduation ceremony.

I know this relocation plan is because of the war and it's meant to help us feel safe. But when I look around, I don't feel safe; I feel sad.

DeeDee —

Trixie was peeved at me for not going to the show with her. "Bud and Eddy might be there," she said. But I had promised Betty I'd come see her.

The person who named it "Camp Harmony" has a warped sense of humor. There is nothing "harmonic" about that place. It's a converted fairgrounds, for crying out loud. My stomach got all nervous when we drove up because there is barbed wire all around the camp. Pop had to show his pass to a guard with a gun at the gate. I've never seen a gun up close before. After we got inside, I asked Pop if the guns were to protect the Japanese, but he didn't answer.

I followed Pop through the camp on wobbly legs. The buildings are arranged by blocks, with bathrooms in each block. People were in lines everywhere — at the mess halls, at the post office, at the bathrooms. I didn't feel right taking pictures of people, so I concentrated on the buildings. I saw why Jim called their place "Knot Inn." Even I could tell the barracks had been thrown together in a hurry. In a couple of places you could see from the outside right into the apartments. They're just big rooms, with no inside walls, so people have hung up blankets to get a little privacy. A little girl peeked her head around a blanket as I was snapping a shot. She was smiling but I didn't see many other smiles today.

Mrs. Tokita isn't very lucky. Her "apartment" is a horse stall — truly! It's dark and smelly, even though she's carted away all the old hay and scrubbed until her knuckles are bleeding. We ate lunch in the mess hall that Betty's family is assigned to. She's right. The food is wretched. It was Vienna sausages and sauerkraut. Betty said that's the third time this week. I'm going to bring a sackful of peanut butter and jelly sandwiches to share next time I come.

I needed to use the facilities while I was there but when I saw the long lines for the latrines — outhouses, really, without any partitions between the wooden seats — I decided to hold it until I got home to our nice, clean bathroom.

But Betty doesn't have that choice.

Wednesday, May 20, 1942

DeeDee —

I wrote Hank about visiting Camp Harmony. I told him about trying to figure out whether the Japanese being sent away for the war was any different than his being sent away for the war, like Bud said. Is it really like rationing, just one more thing we all have to pitch in and do for the war effort?

The thing is, I wonder if Bud would feel that way if he were the one in an assembly center. I couldn't stop thinking about that as I got ready for bed tonight, having a nice, clean bathroom — with a flush toilet! — all to myself and sleeping on a real mattress rather than a cotton sack filled with straw.

Thursday, May 28, 1942

DeeDee —

It's after dinner and my heart is still pounding. I thought we were goners when the air raid siren went off today. One minute I was sitting in Math class and the next minute, I was stumbling out the door, with no time to grab my coat or pocketbook.

"Quietly, children, quietly," our teacher told us. "But quickly."

I found Trixie in the hall. We grabbed hands and kept moving. The hall was crammed with kids on the verge of running and teachers yelling, "Don't run. Don't run."

Miss Mahon's voice on the public address system carried over all the commotion. "This is not a drill. This is a code yellow alert."

Trixie's face turned the same shade of white as her blouse. Code yellow meant we had thirty minutes until the enemy planes showed up. All I could think was, are we the next Pearl Harbor?

"Come on!" I pulled her forward, ignoring our teachers. We ran out of the building, down the steps, and to the street. I looked up at the sky. No planes yet. "My house is closer. Come on!"

"I can't. I can't." Fear glued Trixie to the sidewalk. She was sobbing in great huge gulps. I couldn't waste any more time.

"You have to," I yelled. "Move!" I jerked her so hard she practically fell over. That got her moving, though. I would not let go of her hand, dragging her all those blocks to my front door. I pushed it open and we went flying inside.

Pop came out of the den. The minute I saw him, I burst into tears, too, gasping out the words I'd been carrying in my head all the way home, "It's an air raid."

He ran to the radio and turned it on. Some soap opera was playing. We listened for a few seconds — Trixie and I clinging to each other — and then Pop turned the knob to another station. And another. No emergency announcements. No "We interrupt this program to bring you a special bulletin." It didn't make any sense.

Pop went to the phone. "I'm going to call the school. Piper, why don't you make some hot Ovaltine?"

By the time the milk was warmed, Pop was back in the kitchen with news. "I just got off the phone with the school secretary. It was a drill, girls. Just a drill." He gave Trixie a quick hug then held his arms out to me.

"But they said it was a code yellow." I was shaking again, but I was mad this time.

Trixie started sniffling again. "I thought we were goners."

Pop shook his head. "I don't agree, but the civil defense folks thought it was a good idea to make everyone think it was the real thing." He gave me a squeeze, then stepped away to turn off the flame under the saucepan of milk. He poured it with steady hands into two mugs. I got the Ovaltine out of the cupboard.

"Drink up, you two." He rested his hands on our heads, like he was giving us a blessing. "Trixie, I'll call your mother and let her know you're here."

We drank our Ovaltine and then Mrs. Burke came for Trixie. Pop canceled his church meeting and stayed home with me. I told him he didn't have to.

But I was oh so glad he did.

I never want to go through another day like this again. *Ever.*

Saturday, May 30, 1942

DeeDee —

Pop got six cases of plums from someone at the farmer's market to take to the camp. Fresh fruit is more precious than gold there. I helped him load the crates into the Blue Box with the latest issue of *Modern Screen* from me and a copy of *The Complete Poems of Emily Dickinson* from Miss Wyatt, both for

Betty. I'm betting she'll read the movie magazine first!

No one answered at the Satos' apartment so I left the magazine and book with their neighbor.

Pop and I walked different "avenues" of Area A to hand out fruit. I met an old man and his wife in Section 14, the Matsuis. They didn't go to our church, but I gave them some plums anyway. The man insisted I come in for tea. That's the old Japanese way. If someone gives you a present, you need to give something in return.

The tea tasted like the kind Mrs. Harada always makes. It was nice to have something familiar in this mixed-up place. Mrs. Matsui was in bed, but maybe it was because they only had one chair. A painting of Mt. Rainier hung above the bed. It wasn't picture-perfect, like some art, but there was something about it that made you feel like you were right there, about ready to hike up into the meadows.

I told them how much I liked the painting and Mr. Matsui's face lit up. He started to say something but his wife launched into a coughing fit and couldn't stop. "You'll excuse us, please," he said. He hurried to get her a drink of water. I promised to come back another time and slipped out the door.

Outside, I looked up, over the barbed wire fences, past the guard towers with their machine guns, and beyond the Ferris wheel — left over from the last county fair — and there was Mt. Rainier looming in the distance, etched in white wonder against the blue sky. It doesn't come out from behind the cloud cover very often. I took a picture of it to send to Hank. Though I was looking at the real thing through my viewfinder, I couldn't help thinking about the painting I'd just seen.

And how nobody knew when the people in the camp would be able to see this mountain again from outside that jagged barbed wire fence.

Saturday, June 6, 1942

DeeDee —

When we drove up to Camp Harmony this morning, the guard wouldn't let us through the A gate into Area D. He said Pop's "permanent pass" had expired. Pop asked him how something permanent could expire but the guard wouldn't answer him. All he would say is, "Please remove your vehicle from the premises, sir."

I was scared spitless but not Pop. In his deep, sermon voice, he asked to see the camp commander. The guard pretended he didn't hear him and said, "Please remove your vehicle from the premises, sir." Pop asked again to see the commander, and kept asking. It was like a badminton game, with the shuttlecock being batted back and forth across the net. Only this wasn't a game.

I kept my eyes straight ahead, frozen to the car seat. I was afraid if I looked at the guard, it'd make him even madder. And if I looked at Pop, I might burst into tears. So I studied every detail of the scene through the windshield: the red fence, the tar paper peeling off the roof of the guardhouse, a pair of posters on the side of the small building, one in English and one in Japanese.

Pop and the soldier both stopped talking, each staring the other down. I was hardly able to breathe, because I was sure we were going to get put in jail or worse. Pop didn't blink. It worked! The guard went inside finally and came out with an officer who told Pop he'd have a new pass for him by Tuesday. I never thought of Pop as brave before, but now I see where Hank gets it. Not me. I was still shaking two hours later when we pulled into our own driveway.

Sunday, June 7, 1942

DeeDee —

It's kind of weird not going to our own church. Today we all played hooky again and sat around reading the Sunday papers, which were full of news about a big battle at Midway Island. The papers called it a "great naval-air clash," which ended up being bad for Japan. I found Midway on our globe — it took a magnifying glass to see it way out there in the ocean. I know planes can't fly that far on their own. They're being launched from "bird boats." Like the *Enterprise*.

I read every single word of every single article about the battle and didn't see one mention of which carriers were at Midway.

And it's been weeks since we've heard from Hank.

Monday, June 8, 1942

DeeDee —

Four more days until it's "no more pencils, no more books, no more teachers' dirty looks." Trixie's having a barbecue at her house on Friday night to celebrate the end of seventh grade. Her parents let her invite boys. Eddy will be there, of course. And Bud, too.

He and I made up. He said he was sorry and that he didn't want us to argue anymore. I don't want us to argue, either. But shouldn't I be able to say what I think?

Having a boyfriend is complicated.

Tuesday, June 9, 1942

DeeDee —

At lunch, Eddy said so many of our ships were destroyed at Pearl Harbor that it's a sure bet the *Enterprise* was at Midway. Trixie started chattering about how her party is going. And Bud offered me his last French fry. I know they were trying to distract Eddy and make me feel better. And it worked. For a second. Until Debbie Sue opened her mouth and said her father heard the Japanese were living in luxury, getting all the sugar they wanted, while the rest of us had to make real sacrifices. I got up and walked away from the table. Trixie told me later that I take everything too seriously. That if I didn't try to take the Japanese side all the time, everything would be fine. "You can't change anything about the camps," she said. Which is true. I can't change anything.

But I wish I could.

Wednesday, June 10, 1942

DeeDee —

Pop tried to hide it from me but I saw anyway. Right there on the front page was a report from Tokyo that two U.S. aircraft carriers of the "*Enterprise* and *Hornet* types" had been sunk at Midway.

Maybe Tokyo's lying . . . but maybe they're not.

Thursday, June 11, 1942

DeeDee —

Margie heard some scuttlebutt at work about Midway. But nothing about which ships were involved in the battle.

Friday, June 12, 1942 — The Last Day of Seventh Grade!

DeeDee —

The teachers gave us an hour at the end of the day so we could sign yearbooks. Trixie wrote, "We'll be best friends until Niagara Falls." Debbie Sue wrote, "You and Bud are such a cute couple." Because of my hobby and my report on Margaret Bourke-White, Miss Wyatt wrote, "Use your heart as the true viewfinder." And Bud wrote, "To my favorite shutterbug."

On the way home from school, while Bud was talking about his summer plans, I thought about the autographs that *weren't* in my yearbook — like Betty's. I wondered if any of the other kids at Washington were thinking about our Japanese classmates. It sure didn't seem like it.

Saturday, June 13, 1942

DeeDee —

Trixie's party was a blast! Her mom baked cupcakes and each one had a candy *8* on top, for eighth graders, which is what we are now. We played Crazy

Eights and ate Pieces of Eight (carrot coins) and we danced to all of Trixie's 78s. Since there were more girls than boys at the party, Bud danced with lots of other girls, even Debbie Sue.

I'm only a little bit jealous.

Sunday, June 14, 1942

DeeDee —

Betty's feeling lousy. She says it's the food. I believe it. She wasn't up to visiting today and Pop had business with some of the Nisei men, so I wandered over to Section 14 again. Mr. Matsui was coming back from the mess hall with some hot tea and invited me in. His wife was still in bed. Maybe the food's getting to her, too.

I asked Mr. Matsui about the painting of Mt. Rainier. It turns out that he painted it. He's an artist! But, because they're old and couldn't carry much, he didn't bring any of his supplies with him to camp. When he told me that, his wife got such a sad look on her face.

I got out my camera and asked if I could take a picture of him with his Mt. Rainier. He's so short,

I had to kind of angle the camera up to get both him and the painting in the frame. But I like the way the angle made the mountain look even taller, as tall as it is in real life. Then I said I wanted to take a picture of the two of them. He helped Mrs. Matsui over to their one rickety chair because she didn't want to be photographed in bed. I promised I'd bring them the picture the next time I came.

On the way home in the Blue Box, Pop turned on the radio and we heard a report that one of our aircraft carriers was lost at Midway. Pop's knuckles turned white on the steering wheel and I held my breath while we listened to the rest of the report. I burst into tears when the announcer said it was the *Lexington*. Not the *Enterprise*! Not Hank's ship! Pop pulled over and we said a prayer of thanks right there. Of course, we prayed for all the men on the *Lexington*, too, and their families.

I added a silent prayer of my own: Let us hear from Hank. And soon. This not-knowing is like walking around with a rock in your shoe. Every step hurts. At least with a rock, you can stop and shake it out. There's not one thing I can do about how often we hear from Hank.

Thursday, June 18, 1942

DeeDee —

I try to write Betty every morning. She says that going to the post office for mail is the best part of her day, whether there's mail there or not! She says it's kind of like lunchtime at school—you find your friends and chitchat about what's happened since you saw each other last. "The biggest news here is that there's going to be a wedding in camp. The first," she wrote. "We don't even know the couple but we're going. It'll be something different to do. Mom's sewing the girl an apron and Jim is making them a bookcase. Mikey and Tommy say they're helping but Jim says he could do without their help."

I wrote back and said if she was looking for something to do, she could write to Hank. He loves getting letters; I even have Trixie writing to him now. I put in Hank's address, just in case.

Monday, June 22, 1942

DeeDee —

Hallelujah: a letter from Hank!!!! It was written after the Battle of Midway, on June 8th. I couldn't believe it took so long to get to us but Pop said it's a miracle that in a time of war we're getting any letters at all.

Hank said he out-prayed the chaplain when the fighter planes cleared the *Enterprise* deck because it looked like they might not get off in time. "I know I said I had nine lives, like Admiral," he wrote, "but I was sure glad not to use one up today."

The censors had blacked something out which none of us could read. At the end, he said he was tired and going to hit the sack. After his signature, he wrote, "sism uoy, ripep." I miss him, too.

Pop and I each read it again. It wasn't much of a letter, even by Hank's standards. Not even a paragraph. But that doesn't matter. His sloppy, hunched-over handwriting was more beautiful to me than the finest example of the Palmer method that our Penmanship teachers drilled us on. I don't care how short or sloppy his letters are.

As long as they keep coming.

Tuesday, June 30, 1942

DeeDee —

John writes that he's getting better every day and hopes to start taking some college classes in the fall. He said he was sorry to hear about all the troubles for the Japanese on the coast and to please tell the folks from our church that he's thinking of them, especially Mrs. Harada.

Wednesday, July 1, 1942

DeeDee —

Pop says rumors are for ignoring but Betty's latest letter sounded pretty certain. The assembly centers in California were already sending people to permanent camps. "We hear that the first group from Camp Harmony will be heading to Idaho pretty soon. I can't wait to get out of here. Maybe the sooner we get into those other camps, the sooner we can come home. It's funny, though. Mom feels the opposite. She said, 'Sumeba miyako' — if we stay someplace long enough, it starts to feel like home. But how can hot, rickety wooden barracks ever feel like home?"

Saturday, July 4, 1942

DeeDee —

Bud's family invited me for a Fourth of July picnic at Green Lake. I nearly fell over when Pop said I could go.

Mrs. Greene is very nice. And so stylish in her trousers and blouse. She looks like Katharine Hepburn. Mr. Greene has this funny, loud laugh. And he laughs a lot. After a picnic of bologna sandwiches and potato chips, he gave us some money to walk to the concession stand for ice cream. As soon as we were out of sight of his parents, Bud took my hand.

"It's going to be hard to take pictures this way," I teased.

"I'll let you go when you find something worth shooting," he told me. It does make you think twice about whether a picture's worth taking when your hand is all warm and safe in someone else's. But I did get a great shot of ten turtles sunning themselves on a log at the lake's edge, and a little girl walking an enormous Saint Bernard, and what I think will be my favorite: an old couple sitting on a bench sharing a bag of peanuts with the squirrels.

This was the nicest day I can remember in a long, long time.

Sunday, July 5, 1942

DeeDee —

Mr. R. L. Nicholson, who's the director of the Federal Works Agency for the western states, was quoted in the *Times* today. "It is mere conjecture, of course, but I would say 90–95 percent of the internees are quite content to remain in custody."

I don't exactly know what conjecture means and I don't feel like looking it up. I am on summer vacation, after all. I've been to Camp Harmony — twice now — and I would say that nobody there was content with being behind those barbed wire fences.

Friday, July 10, 1942

DeeDee —

A short letter from Hank. He said he'd realized he'd never answered my question from a few letters back, the question about the difference between him being sent away because of the war and the Japanese being sent away because of the war.

Sis, that's a big question you're asking and the kind of thing people have to work out for themselves. (Boy, I sound like the old man there, don't I?) For what it's worth, the way I see it is that I volunteered for the Navy, knowing there was a possibility I'd be sent into action in case of war. The people who are being sent away now didn't volunteer to go, that's for sure. You bet we all have to sacrifice during wartime. But people in the camps are giving up more than sugar or gasoline or new tires. Gosh, I've turned this into a sermon, haven't I? Guess I really do take after Pop. Don't take any wooden nickels. — Hank.

I like the way Hank explains things. It makes sense to me.

I wish it made sense to all those other people who think the camps are a good idea.

Sunday, July 12, 1942

DeeDee —

Betty is spitting mad at Jim. "All he has to do is fill out some paperwork and he can get permission to leave the camp to go away to college. Just think — no more lines at the bathroom, no more mess hall food, no more wasting time going to the pretend school they've set up here in camp. And who knows what it will be like in Idaho? But he won't do it! He says with Dad gone, he's the man of the family. He can't leave us. Mom and I can handle things. He is making a huge mistake. Missing a big chance." There were indentations in the paper, she'd been writing so hard. "Can you please ask your father to talk to him next time he comes down? Maybe he will listen to him."

I showed the letter to Pop and he said he would talk to Jim but he wasn't sure it would do any good.

Tuesday, July 14, 1942

DeeDee —

It's Margie's 21st birthday today! I baked her a sheet cake, which was only a little lumpy. And John even called long-distance from Minnesota to sing to her. She looked pleased with her gifts—a bottle of Joy perfume from me and a new wrench for her work toolbox from Pop—but had to hurry off for her shift at Boeing. She was smiling, though, so I think we cheered her up a little bit, even though I know she's missing Stan something awful. His unit was sent to England right after basic training; we know that much but nothing about what he's doing there. The last she heard from him he had a rotten cold because June in England is like November in Seattle. Margie sent him three pairs of wool socks after he wrote her that his biggest problem isn't the Nazis but keeping his feet dry.

When she blew out her candles, I made a wish, too: that Stan would be home to celebrate her next birthday.

Hank, too.

Friday, July 17, 1942

DeeDee —

Pop went to Camp Harmony today to talk to Jim about signing up for college so he could leave the camp.

Pop was right. It didn't do any good.

Sunday, July 19, 1942

DeeDee —

I spent the night last night with Trixie and went to church with her family this morning. I'm glad we're not Lutheran — there was a lot of standing up and sitting down.

In the afternoon, we went roller-skating with Bud and Eddy. I was sure Pop would say no, but he's been so distracted lately that I didn't even have to beg.

After skating, we went to Woolworth's and had sodas. Bud and I shared a strawberry one — with two straws. It wasn't as romantic as they make it look in the movies but it was still fun. The best part was the strawberry kiss good-bye!

Monday, July 20, 1942

DeeDee —

Pop's all in a dither because he has to take a trip on church business to California, to visit the Pinedale Assembly Center near Fresno and the WRA camp at Tule Lake. He's not in a dither about the trip, of course. He wants to go because he feels it will "light a fire" under the denomination headquarters about doing more for the Japanese. Since he doesn't have a church of his own anymore, this has become his job.

What has him worried is what to do with me. I have told him a million times I'll be fine. Margie works nights, which is when I'm sleeping. Miss McCullough lives two blocks over and I can always call Trixie's mom in a pinch.

Margie finally convinced him that everything would be jake for us girls on our own.

I wrote Betty all about it that night. "I don't think Pop is ever going to stop treating me like a child." Without thinking, I wrote, "Does your dad treat you like that, too?" That was a crummy thing to put in, with Betty's dad in the prison camp so far away. So I scratched that out and ended with, "Speaking of kids, I have a new joke for Mikey and

Tommy. What did the dog say when he rubbed his tail on sandpaper? Ruff. Ruff."

I signed off as I always did: LLL — Longer Letter Later.

Thursday, July 23, 1942

DeeDee —

Margie was still at work, so I got up and fixed Pop a good breakfast before he hit the road. The toast wasn't burned and the eggs were over easy, just the way he likes them. I followed Margie's instructions for making coffee. I tried it and it tasted disgusting to me but Pop had two cups so I did all right. I wrapped up some sandwiches in waxed paper and poured the rest of the coffee into his thermos.

The house was so quiet after he left. And it seemed too big, too. Instead of feeling grown-up, I felt like a little kid again. Like a four-year-old who needed to be rocked to sleep. It didn't help when Margie got home. She ate a couple of eggs and some toast, took a hot bath, and went to bed.

I read my new library book on photography, baked a batch of oatmeal cookies, and wrote letters to John, Stan, and Hank. I added a P.S. to Hank's: "hisw uoy eerw eerh."

Being on your own isn't all it's cracked up to be.

Sunday, July 26, 1942

DeeDee —

Bud can't come over while Pop's gone, but he's called every day. He asked if I could go on a bike ride with him, Eddy, and Trixie, but Margie said no. Trixie went, which would have been something to see. She hardly ever does anything that requires muscles!

Monday, August 10, 1942

DeeDee —

Pastor Thomson stopped by to see how we were doing. His wife sent along a casserole and a blueberry cobbler for us. Quite an improvement over Margie's cooking.

Pastor Thomson says the rumors are true. Most of the people in Camp Harmony are going to a War Relocation Camp in Idaho, called Minidoka. A group of men left today to get it ready for everyone.

He didn't know if Jim was in the group. And

he didn't know when people were going to start leaving.

Maybe the war will end and nobody else will have to go to Minidoka.

Wednesday, August 12, 1942

DeeDee —

Another letter from Betty. "Well, the last of the camp movie projectors is now broken beyond repair. No more movie nights. The movie selection wasn't that great, but it was still better than nothing. Even a bad movie helps me forget about this place, if only for an hour or so."

Saturday, August 15, 1942

DeeDee —

Margie gave the okay for me to go with Trixie and the gang to Lake Washington to swim. We met up at Collins Playfield and walked together from there to Mount Baker Beach. It was a hot day and the water felt cool. Bud found a beach ball that someone left behind and we played a game of water volleyball, boys against girls. Once when I was going up for a smash, Bud snuck around and dunked me, making me miss my shot. I said that was no fair and he said all was fair in love and war. Then I dunked him for saying that. On the way home, we walked the woods trail, picking blackberries and hazelnuts. The boys got into a berry fight but that stopped when Eddy got Trixie smack on the forehead. I took pictures of everybody on the swings at the playfield before we all headed home.

This is one of those days, though, that I won't need a picture of to remember.

Sunday, August 16, 1942

DeeDee —

Pop's home! I took a picture of him getting his briefcase out of the Blue Box. Then I gave him a big hug. I'd really missed him.

"Was it a good trip?" I asked. "Did they listen to you?"

He handed me his briefcase and reached into the backseat for his suitcase. "It was very worthwhile. I think progress is being made."

Margie came out and grabbed his bag. "You look bushed, Pop. Come on in. Are you hungry?"

He said he'd eaten in Tacoma and was fine. He patted the Blue Box's front fender. "Another thousand miles on this old crate. I sure hope the tires hold out."

We went inside and he had a cup of coffee and we had tea. "So was it a worthwhile trip?" Margie asked.

Pop smiled tiredly. "Let's say, they gave me tentative approval for a new plan I have."

"And what's that?" Margie asked.

"Too early to share." Pop yawned big. "I have a few phone calls to make and then I've got to catch up on some shut-eye."

He did look beat, but it would've been nice to hear a little more about his trip. Not the business part, but the travel part. I wanted to know if Mt. Shasta was as beautiful in person as it was in pictures, and to hear about the people he'd met along the way.

I know his work is important but sometimes I wish he could be Pop first and Pastor Davis second.

At least he made it home for my big day.

Monday, August 17, 1942

DeeDee —

Happy Birthday to me! Trixie gave me a teeny tiny camera charm to start my own charm bracelet, like the one she wears. Now I have to get the bracelet! Bud gave me a roll of film and two Sky Bars; Margie gave me a new twinset — green, to set off my brown eyes; and Betty sent me a birthday card she'd made. But Pop's present was the best of all. He took Margie and me out to the Dog House for Crab Louies. He even let me order a Shirley Temple and the waiter brought it with fourteen cherries floating in the glass — one for each year.

Guess what I wished for when I blew out the candle on my piece of chocolate cake!?

If I tell you, it might not come true.

Thursday, August 20, 1942

DeeDee —

It was a regular landslide of letters today. Besides the ones Pop's always getting from people in Tule Lake or Pinedale or Camp Harmony, there were letters from

Hank, Stan, and John. Margie wouldn't let me read the one from Stan — it probably had lots of mushy stuff in it — but she said he'd won $10 in a poker game. He was going to send it to her but then he met a little English girl who didn't have a coat, which she really needed because England is damp and cold, even in the summer. So he bought her one, and a hat, too. Telling that story got Margie all choked up.

John is all signed up for classes for the fall. He said Pop inspired him to take a course in philosophy and that I inspired him to take a course in photography. Pretty neat.

Hank's letter didn't say much. Which is good, because that way the censor didn't mark it all up! At the end, he wrote, "yapph yirthdab ot ym dik ristes."

I wrote back, "ton hucs a dik — mi nourteef!"

Friday, August 21, 1942

DeeDee —

Section B cleared out of Camp Harmony today, the first group to leave for Idaho. Pop said as bad as Harmony is, people acted sad to leave it. At least they knew what to expect there. No one has any idea of what they'll be going to in Minidoka.

I don't know when Betty and her family will be sent to Idaho.

Neither does she.

Thursday, August 27, 1942

DeeDee —

I was all set to go school shopping with Trixie and her mom when the call came. The Satos were leaving Camp Harmony. Today! Pop and I hopped in the Blue Box and made it down to Puyallup in the nick of time to say good-bye.

Mikey and Tommy were all excited about getting to ride on the train. They were running around, hollering "choo-choo" as loud as they could. I gave them each a roll of Neccos for the long overnight trip — but they immediately started gobbling them up. I tried! Betty and Jim were as quiet as their little brothers were noisy. Betty thanked me for the care package I'd brought for her — three movie magazines, a deck of playing cards, and two Sky Bars. We stood there, waiting without talking. When it was time to board the train, Jim took Mikey's hand and Betty took Tommy's. They followed their mother up the steps and, in a blink, were lost inside the dark of the car.

I know it doesn't make any sense, because the train car windows were all blacked out — we couldn't see in and Betty and her family couldn't see out — but Pop and I stood there, waving until the train was an ant on the tracks.

Saturday, August 29, 1942

DeeDee —

I broke open my piggy bank and cleaned Mrs. Lee's grocery out of penny candy. Margie and Pop helped me divvy the treats up into paper sacks and then we drove down and handed them out to all the little kids still at Camp Harmony.

Maybe that will sweeten the long trip to Idaho a little bit.

Monday, September 7, 1942

DeeDee —

I start eighth grade tomorrow. Next year, we'll be lowly freshmen so I plan to enjoy every minute of being an eighth-grade "top dog." Trixie wants us to go out for the Girls' Club, but I have my eye on the school newspaper. I'm sure they need a crack photographer!

Tuesday, September 8, 1942

DeeDee —

This is going to be such a great year. I like all of my teachers — well, as much as you can like them after one day of classes. We get to sit at the eighth-grade table in the cafeteria, and Miss Wyatt is the newspaper club advisor and she was so happy that I wanted to be the photographer.

I was so bubbly on the way home from school that Bud said he was going to start calling me "Soda Pop"!

Wednesday, September 9, 1942

DeeDee —

I hate, hate, hate my father! And I don't care if that gets me sent to h-e-double-toothpicks.

Tonight after supper, Pop said he had something to tell me. I said okay. I'd been hearing bits and pieces and figured it was probably about his new church assignment.

"Mr. Carter at the denomination headquarters has given his blessing to the plan I'd mentioned back in August." Pop smiled. "In fact, he paid me quite a compliment. Said I was the man for the job."

"That's great, Pop." I innocently took a bite of apple crisp, completely unaware of what was coming next.

Pop cleared his throat. "We're moving," he said. "To Minidoka."

I dropped my fork. "Where? No. No."

"Well, we won't be allowed to live in the camp. Only WRA folks can. But we can stay there until we find a place nearby. Maybe Hunt or Eden or Twin Falls."

I thought of Bud and Trixie and everything. "Pop, all my friends are here."

"Betty's your friend," he said. He took a bite of his apple crisp and chewed calmly, as if he wasn't ruining his youngest daughter's life.

I looked down at my own plate. I wanted to throw it. I wanted to hear it crash against the wall, shattering into pieces. I wanted to throw all of the plates. I didn't, but I shoved my chair back from the table, shouting and sobbing at the same time. "You don't care about me. Not one bit. All you care about is the Japanese." I practically growled in anger and frustration. I threw my fork and then my napkin down on the table. "I hate you!"

Pop set his own fork and napkin down slowly. Carefully. "I can imagine you aren't very happy with me right now, Piper. But the decision is made. Now, you may go to your room. I will clean up the dishes. We can talk more after you've calmed down."

I turned around so hard I knocked the chair over. And I didn't stop to pick it up. I ran up to my room, slammed my bedroom door, and threw myself on the bed, pounding the pillows as hard as I could.

He's the pastor, not me, so I don't know why I have to go to Idaho. It's not like I can do anything to help.

I'm *not* going to move.

Thursday, September 10, 1942

DeeDee —

He can't make me do this.

Friday, September 11, 1942

DeeDee —

Trixie had a brilliant idea. She said I should ask Pop if I could live with her family while he goes to Idaho;

after all, it can't be for very long, right? That way, I could help Margie keep an eye on the house. And Pop could do his important work without having me underfoot. It was the perfect solution!

I helped Margie make Pop's favorite dinner, goulash. I set the table without complaining once, and the second Pop's coffee cup got empty, I jumped up to fill it up.

"Thank you for dinner, girls." Pop dabbed his mouth with his napkin and started to stand up.

"Pop, wait. I have something to ask you." I nervously smoothed out my skirt.

He cocked his head like our neighbor's spaniel. "Okay."

I glanced over at Margie. She took the hint. "I'm going to go wash my hair." She carried her plate to the kitchen and then went upstairs.

I cleared my throat. "I was talking to Trixie and she said, well, she asked her mom and *she* said it was okay . . ."

"I'm not following you, Piper."

I started again. "Can I live with Trixie while you're gone? It's okay with her mom and dad. That way I wouldn't have to change schools when classes have already started."

"That's very generous of the Burkes," Pop said.

My heart beat double-time and I sat up straighter. Trixie's plan worked!

"But the answer is no."

I slumped down in my chair. "But why not?" I hated the little kid whiny tone in my voice but I couldn't help it.

"We couldn't impose on the Burkes like that." He took off his glasses and rubbed the bridge of his nose. "I don't even know how long we'll be in Idaho."

"But it wouldn't be imposing. Trixie said so. And couldn't Margie use some help with the house?"

"I've given my answer, Piper." I started to say something else but he held up his hand. "I don't want to hear any more about it."

Well, he won't have to.

I am never speaking to him again.

Saturday, September 12, 1942

DeeDee —

I'm being shook up by an earthquake full of bad news. On top of Pop's announcement, there's war news from the Pacific. The Navy and the Marines are duking it out with the Japanese over these tiny little specks called the Solomon Islands. I found them on our globe, east of Australia and New Guinea. We have no way of knowing for sure, but we all worry that the *Enterprise* is there.

I wrote Hank a long letter tonight and signed it, "eb rupes-ruped larefuc!!!"

Monday, September 14, 1942

DeeDee —

On the way home from school today, I broke the news to Bud. I could hardly hold back my tears and I thought he was pretty broken up, too, because he didn't say a word for blocks. When we got to my house, he reached for my hand. The September sun lit up the maple leaves behind his head so that it looked like he was wearing a crown. He looked at me with those green eyes of his. Then he took a deep breath and I was certain he was going to pledge me his undying love, like the hero did in that last pirate movie we saw. I got all shaky and started crying even harder.

Then he said, "Well, I've been thinking we should see other people, anyway."

That stopped my tears right away. How could he be so heartless? Couldn't he see how sad I was?

"I guess I'd never seen the real you before," I said. My voice was quavery, but I summoned up all the dignity I could. I pretended I was Joan Fontaine finally standing up to the evil housekeeper in the movie *Rebecca*. "I'll give your pin back, of course."

"Okay. Thanks." Bud smiled at me. I never noticed that he had crooked front teeth. What had I ever seen in him, besides those green eyes?

I straightened my back and walked away, down the sidewalk, alone, leaving my first true love behind.

It can't get any worse than this.

Tuesday, September 15, 1942

DeeDee —

More doom. More gloom.

Still not speaking to Pop.

Thursday, September 17, 1942

DeeDee —

One crumb of good news. A postcard from Hank. The *Enterprise* had taken some "body punches" near the Solomon Islands and was headed some-where — name of the place had been cut out by a censor — to get patched up. The crew gets a month's leave in Pearl Harbor while repairs are being made. I wish he could come home but I am still thankful.

One month away from the fighting for my brother — glory hallelujah!

Monday, September 21, 1942

DeeDee —

As Trixie was helping me clean out my locker, Bud walked by, Debbie Sue at his side.

I caught Trixie looking at me, and knew she was wondering what to say. Even though I felt like I'd gotten the wind knocked out of me, I wasn't going to let anyone know.

"*That* didn't take long," I said, in as flip a tone as I could muster.

Trixie gave me another look, and then grabbed me in a hug. "You deserve better, that's for sure."

What would we do without our friends?!

Wednesday, September 23, 1942

DeeDee —

The last group left Camp Harmony today. Pop's loading up our things in the Blue Box. Margie helped pack up the kitchen and the bedding and Pop's books.

She dropped some empty cardboard boxes in my bedroom. I kicked them in the corner.

If she can stay, I don't see why I can't.

Thursday, September 24, 1942

DeeDee —

When I turn eighteen, I am going to do whatever I want to do. Wear lipstick every day. Go to any movie I want. And live wherever I want.

Which will not be Podunk Town, Idaho, U.S.A.

Friday, September 25, 1942

DeeDee —

Of all the low blows, this is the lowest. Without telling me, Margie wrote to Hank about the move and my "childish" reaction. Leave it to Margie to get to him before I had a chance to tell my side of the story. He wrote to say he's disappointed to learn I've been giving Pop a hard time. "People all over the world are making sacrifices. That's what happens in war. You need to just 'grin and bear it,' for Pop's sake."

I fumed after reading it.

Why doesn't anyone have to do anything for Piper's sake?

Saturday, September 26, 1942

DeeDee —

Trixie never gets up before ten on Saturdays but she was here at 5 A.M., with red eyes and a bag of doughnuts. We both cried and promised to write. It was the hardest thing to open the car door and climb in. I leaned out the window and waved until I couldn't see her anymore.

There were two apple fritters in the bag — Pop's favorites.

I ate them both.

Minidoka
War Relocation
Center

Eden, Idaho

Monday, September 28, 1942

DeeDee —

It takes one and a half days to drive from 307 Spruce Street, Seattle, Washington, to the Minidoka War Relocation Center, near Eden, Idaho. I did not say a single word the entire way except "Please pass the salt" when we stopped for supper last night.

Pop didn't even seem to notice.

Tuesday, September 29, 1942

DeeDee —

I couldn't write last night about the camp. It's worse than I ever imagined. The same kind of joker who named Camp Harmony must have named the town of Eden. I can't imagine a place less like paradise. The heat is bad enough but it's the dust that really gets to you. There are gaps around the windows and doors and even in the walls so the dust blows right in. No amount of sweeping gets it up. I've already got a sore throat from breathing it and this is only our first day.

There are latrines here, too, and lines to use them, like Camp Harmony. I took my flashlight and went around 11 P.M. and I was the only one there, thank goodness. I knew from Betty to spray a hanky with the smelliest perfume possible and hold it to my nose. These outhouses weren't built to be used by so many people! The camp manager says real bathrooms are coming but doesn't say when.

If Pop had his way, we'd live here, right in the camp. But since he's "just" a minister and doesn't work for the WRA, it's against the rules. Thank goodness. We can stay until we find a place nearby to rent. Pop and I went into Eden to look around and found one house that might've worked. The landlord was real friendly to us until he asked what line of work Pop was in.

"The Lord's work," Pop answered. "I'm a Baptist minister."

"I'm not much of a churchgoer myself," the man said. "But I didn't know the old preacher had left."

"I'm not serving a congregation here in town," Pop said. "My congregation's over at Hunt."

As soon as Pop said that, I knew it was a mistake. The man shifted back, as if trying to avoid smelling something unpleasant.

"Hunt? Nothing there but that camp." The man walked over to the front door and opened it. "My son was at Pearl Harbor. I don't rent to no Jap lovers."

When the door slammed behind us, I called back over my shoulder, "My brother was at Pearl Harbor, too!"

But the door stayed firmly shut.

Wednesday, September 30, 1942

DeeDee —

Pop had business with the camp manager today so I'm waiting around in the waiting room (get it?!) in the guard house. The only nice part of the room is the fireplace, which one of the guards told me is made from stones they got from the desert. There isn't much else to look at in here. Not like at my dentist where I can at least look at the *Reader's Digest* magazine. There's one photo on the wall. It's of the camp, taken from a plane. In the picture, the buildings look like a cock-eyed capital *M*, kind of like this:

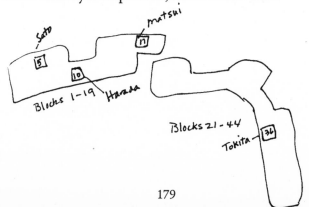

Pop's still busy. Maybe I should describe the camp a bit, though there's not much chance of me forgetting what this place looks like, even when I'm an old lady. To get here, you take State Highway 25. You turn off on a road—I don't know the name of it—and drive over a bridge that spans the Twin Falls canal. It's different than Camp Harmony because there's only one gate here. Once you're inside the gate, there are two roads. The one to the left takes you to the MPs (Military Police), the hospital, and Blocks 1-19; you go straight ahead to get to Blocks 21-44.

This place is huge. I should know. We have to park the Blue Box at the gate and it takes forever to walk places. Luckily, Betty's in Block 5. That's not as far as some of the other blocks. Mrs. Harada is in Block 10, the Matsuis in Block 17, but Mrs. Tokita is way over in Block 36.

Each block has twelve barracks, a mess hall—oops, I mean dining hall (the camp manager won't let anybody call it a mess hall)—and a social hall. Between the two rows of barracks, there's an H-shaped building with the laundry and bathrooms. Well, it's where the bathrooms will be when they get real bathrooms. Here's a not-very-good picture:

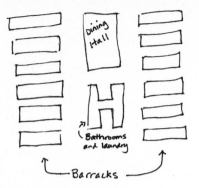

Right now, we're staying in one of the staff apartments, behind the administration building, by the gate. It's nicer than the barracks but I can't wait to get into a real house of our own.

Thursday, October 1, 1942

DeeDee —

We've been here less than a week and it feels like a year. Today's dinner was a pork chop with fried apples. It looked tasty. But looks are deceiving. The minute I put a bite in my mouth, I was chewing grit along with the food. The dust here gets into absolutely everything. My teeth ache all the time. It's like having a serving of sandpaper with every meal. Jim Sato says it's our "DIDD" — "Daily Involuntary Dose of Dust."

I'd take Margie's meat loaf over this any day.

Sunday, October 4, 1942

DeeDee —

Today was Pop's first church service in camp. You'd have to use your imagination to see that barracks room as a church, but the people who came didn't seem to mind. One of the moms even had a sort of Sunday school class in the back for the little kids who couldn't sit through church.

Until Miss McCullough arrives in a few weeks, I am Pop's assistant. Which means I help set up the chairs, pass out the hymnals, and make sure he has a glass of water on his makeshift pulpit. It's a good thing I don't know how to play the piano, or I'd be the accompanist, too.

Betty took that temporary job. I wouldn't tell Miss McCullough, of course, but Betty's better at playing the piano than she is. I can actually tell which hymn we're supposed to be singing when Betty plays!

Monday, October 5, 1942

DeeDee —

Hot dogs for lunch. Bologna for dinner.

Pop and I had Alka-Seltzer for "dessert."

Wednesday, October 7, 1942

DeeDee —

This is our last night in the camp! Pop found a house and we're moving in tomorrow. My bedroom is done all in yellow and is tucked in a dormer under the roof. Mrs. Harada says that as soon as her sewing machine comes, she'll make me some gingham curtains for the windows. I broke my vow of silence to tell Pop how much I loved it. Honestly, it's even nicer than my room at home. I took lots of photos to send to Hank, along with our new address: 339 Second Avenue North, Twin Falls, Idaho.

Betty was happy for us, but I felt bad telling her. She has to share one room with three brothers, her mother, a dresser, and five beds. Well, *beds* is an optimistic word. They're canvas cots with lumpy mattresses. I didn't tell her about the rosebud wallpaper or the window seat where I can curl up and read.

Friday, October 9, 1942

DeeDee —

Pop told me to ignore him, but it's pretty hard to ignore a grown man standing on the sidewalk, staring at the house.

Mr. Crofton owns the café downtown. It all started when we went in for lunch today. Pop heard they served good patty melts. The waitress showed us to a booth and handed us menus but before she could take our order, Mr. Crofton was there, grabbing the menus out of our hands. "I don't serve your kind in here," he said.

"What kind is that?" Pop asked. "The hungry kind?"

"Don't give me any lip. I know what you do. And I ain't gonna have you in here stinking up the place."

I don't know how Pop can stay so calm. I was shaking like a wet cat. Somehow, I was able to stand up and follow Pop out of the café. "There's egg salad at home," he said. "That'll be tasty, won't it?"

All I could do was nod and wobble home behind him. We'd gone about a block when I realized Mr. Crofton was tailing us. When we got to our house, he stopped on the sidewalk across the street, just staring.

We made lunch and ate it. He is still out there.

Pop said not to pay him any mind. To go about my business. I went upstairs to write some letters to Hank and Trixie, but couldn't help peeking out my curtains.

I saw Mr. Crofton bend down and pick up a rock. He stood there, tossing it up and down, up and down in his hand.

I want to go home.

Saturday, October 10, 1942

DeeDee —

The first thing I did when I woke up was look out my window.

No Mr. Crofton standing on the sidewalk.

For now.

Sunday, October 11, 1942

DeeDee —

Another rainy day. We brought two boxes of oranges to camp to give to people after services. Between the dust and the change in the weather, nearly everyone in camp has caught cold. Pop thought the oranges might help. It was freezing on the ride over because the heater's quit working in the Blue Box. I went with Pop to visit the Satos — it was even colder than being in the Blue Box. Their apartment still doesn't have a stove. It wouldn't do them that much good if they had one. There's not enough coal to go around.

On the way home in the car, Pop talked to me about school. He's actually giving me a choice. The school in Twin Falls or the one at the camp, which won't open until next month.

Getting an extra vacation or starting school right away?

That was easy as pie to decide.

Monday, October 12, 1942

DeeDee —

A bunch of the high school kids signed up to help with the sugar beet harvest. I watched a truck come get them this morning. Jim and his buddy Yosh Nakata went. So did Betty. She said they used to help on their grandparents' farm every summer. She didn't mind the work.

Then she looked wistfully across the barbed wire fencing and said at least helping with the harvest would get her out of camp for a bit.

A little taste of freedom.

Wednesday, October 14, 1942

DeeDee —

We heard from John that he likes two things about college: his history class and the girl who sits in front of him in his history class. "I haven't got up the gumption to ask her name," he wrote, "but I will."

Friday, October 16, 1942

DeeDee —

Mr. Crofton's back. Pop says it's only whiskey talking but he's out there yelling stuff at us. Some of the words I've never even heard before.

Part of me thinks he's acting like a little kid who can't get his own way and is throwing a temper tantrum. But that's only a small part. The rest of me is terrified of what might happen next. Maybe the whiskey will make him do more than cuss at us. I try not to think about what had happened to Mr. Tokita but I can't help it. No matter how cheerful my yellow room is, it isn't a comfort anymore.

I want Pop to call the police but he says we need to turn the other cheek.

Saturday, October 17, 1942

DeeDee —

We took the Satos some extra blankets this afternoon so we were there when Betty and Jim came back from helping with the harvest. Jim was wearing a shiner. His face was banged up pretty good.

Pop asked him what happened. He didn't answer but grabbed a towel and said he was going to wash up. Betty burst into tears the minute he left the room. It turns out that the farmer had told his sons to move their sorry rear ends. He pointed out that they outweighed Jim by about 50 pounds but he was lifting 100-pound sugar beet sacks on his own. The farmer said it in front of the whole crew. So the boys waited until Jim was in the far field, all by himself, and jumped him. To teach him a lesson. Betty said she wasn't going back. And she didn't want Jim to, either.

Mrs. Sato's hands shook as she served us all some tea. When Jim came back in the room, he drank two cups, real fast. He must've known that Betty told us what happened because he set his cup down and said, "I'm not quitting. Then they'll think they've won."

Nobody said anything. Because we all knew it was true.

Monday, October 19, 1942

DeeDee —

Just like he said he would be, Jim was on the farm truck. Betty and Yosh, too. They said they weren't going to let him go alone, no matter what. Betty told me later that those two farm boys tried to pull their tricks on Jim again. But this big guy from Eden managed to be Jim's shadow all day. So the farmer's sons left him alone.

Tuesday, October 20, 1942

DeeDee —

On my way to visit the Matsuis today, I stopped to help Mrs. Harada plant tumbleweed by her doorway. All around camp, people are making cactus and sagebrush gardens, ringing them with lava rocks. As scrubby as they are, the gardens look hopeful somehow.

I took a picture of Mr. Matsui with the watercolors and paper I brought him from town. It felt really good to see his wife smile, too. She even sat up in bed so he could show her all the colors. He said he was going to paint a garden for his wife. Something cheerful to look at while she was getting better.

Then he said something to me in Japanese that I didn't understand. But I could tell it was something nice from the way they were both looking at me.

Wednesday, October 21, 1942

DeeDee —

Nothing but wind and dust. I helped Mrs. Harada clean her floor. First, we tore old newspapers into thin strips, then we sprinkled the strips with water from a small watering can. We scattered the papers over the floor and let them sit for a bit. They were like dust magnets, loaded with dust instead of metal shavings, when we swept them up. The thing is, once we swept up one batch of paper, more dust would settle.

"It's hopeless," I told her. "The dust comes right back!"

Mrs. Harada shrugged. "*Shikata ga nai*. It cannot be helped. If I want a clean floor, I must sweep."

I looked around her room. It was neat as a pin.

A handmade quilt lay across her Army cot bed. One of the neighbors in Block 8 built her a desk and bench out of scrap wood. It was pushed against the wall, in the corner, opposite the bed. The tea set Mr. Harada gave her last Christmas sat on top of the desk. Last time I'd been over, she'd made us tea. But not in that set. She said she wasn't going to use it until she could make tea for Mr. Harada.

A few letters leaned against the teapot. I could make out the Fort Missoula postmark and a black stamp that said, "Detained Alien Enemy Mail." Mrs. Harada saw me looking at them. "I haven't heard from him in a while. He has been writing everyone he can think of—the state attorney general, the U.S. attorney general—to request another hearing. He can only write so many letters each week so maybe he's used up his limit on that business." She leaned the broom in the corner. "I can miss a few letters if it means he will be able to come here sooner. So we can be together sooner." She opened her arms and I stepped into her hug. "Thank you for helping," she said. When I was little, she would hug me when I was sad, pretending to squeeze me so hard, she'd squeeze the sad out.

"I wish I could squeeze your sad out," I said.

She patted my cheek. "You are a good girl, Piper." As I was leaving, she grabbed the broom and started sweeping again.

Every day, when I get home from the camp, I rinse out my mouth but can't ever get all the grit out. I'll be chewing on sand until I'm a hundred.

Thursday, October 22, 1942
DeeDee —

A new group of "colonists" arrived today. That's what the camp manager calls the Japanese. It's always the same. They show up dressed in their very best clothes, like they were going to church or to a party. After a day or so, they're wearing old clothes, like everyone else. The dust ruins everything, even what we wear on our backs.

Friday, October 23, 1942
DeeDee —

Mr. Crofton's outside again tonight. So far, he's standing there, staring at the house. But there's a brown paper bag in his hand. I know that means that pretty soon he'll start up with the yelling.

I don't even really hear him anymore.

Saturday, October 24, 1942

DeeDee —

Today was the last day of the sugar beet harvest. I ate supper in the dining hall with Jim, Yosh, and Betty and heard all about it.

Jim said that big guy who'd stood up with him was named Dean. "He always managed to be on my crew. Worked next to me every day. He didn't say anything, didn't really talk. And at lunch, he'd take his sandwich and sit off by himself. But he was always in range." Jim stopped to take a sip of tea.

"If Dean was in a movie, he would definitely play one of the bad guys," Yosh added.

"The bad guy with a good heart," Jim said. "So all of harvest Dean doesn't say boo to me. Then today, as we're all getting cleaned up to head back to camp, he comes over. He says he used to be as thickheaded as anybody about the Japanese but that working with me had changed his mind."

Betty jumped in. "He said that anybody who

worked as hard as Jim was his kind of people. He shook Jim's hand, right in front of everyone."

I sat there for a minute, trying to picture the scene. "I wish I could've been there," I said.

"Let me tell you," Jim said. "It made that shiner worth it."

I said I was sure it did.

Sunday, October 25, 1942

DeeDee —

One of the chefs from the dining hall in 17 was fired for stealing some chickens to cook for himself and his friends instead of for the "colonists." They need to fire the rest of them, too, not because they're stealing but because not one of them can cook.

After church, I stopped to see Mr. and Mrs. Matsui. She looked better, I thought. Maybe it was because of the brand-new watercolor painting of the sunflower fields hanging on the wall across from the bed, where she could see it.

Monday, October 26, 1942

DeeDee —

Glory and hallelujah! They've promised real bath-rooms by November 1st.

Watchtowers are going up at the edge of the camp. Some people say they're fire lookouts but others say they're going to be for soldiers with machine guns. So no one can escape. As if there was anywhere to go in this place of never-ending desert.

Wednesday, October 28, 1942

DeeDee —

The "colonists" can now apply for passes to go to town. Betty got one, and Pop brought her into Twin Falls so the two of us could shop for prizes for the Halloween carnival coming up. It was a lot of fun — as long as we avoided the stores and cafés like Mr. Crofton's that said NO JAPS. There weren't many of them; most of the people were nice to us. The lady at the five-and-ten-cent store had as much fun as we did picking out prizes the little kids would like.

"Oh, you've got to have marbles," she'd say. Or, "What's a party without noisemakers?" Or, "That's not near enough penny candy." When we showed her how much we had to spend, she said, "That'll cover it. No problem."

We walked out of there with sacks of prizes in our hands and big smiles on our faces. It was nice to be reminded there are lots more people like her in the world than there are Mr. Croftons.

Friday, October 30, 1942

DeeDee —

Cold and windy and the Satos still don't have a stove. This morning, I helped Betty, Jim, and Yosh drag over a bunch of sagebrush and we started a fire out by their road. It was smelly and smoky but better than being an ice cube.

School still hasn't started. It's set to open in a few weeks. I thought I'd have a bit of vacation, but Pop had other ideas. He's kept me busy typing up his sermons and the letters of recommendation he gets asked to write. He says typing is a valuable skill and I'll be thankful for all this practice some-day. I doubt it! What I would be thankful for is a typewriter that corrected mistakes. I wish someone would hurry up and invent one.

Saturday, October 31, 1942 — Halloween

DeeDee —

The Halloween carnival was a huge hit with the little kids. Jim and Yosh found a big cardboard box somewhere and painted it to look like a cave. They put it at the entrance to the social hall so the kids had to crawl through it to get into the party. There were three different sections: the haunted house — complete with peeled grape "eyeballs" and spaghetti-in-ketchup "innards" — a carnival, and refreshments.

Betty and I ran the goldfish booth in the carnival section. Mikey came over, munching a doughnut.

"I want a harmonica," he said.

"Well, you'll have to be a good fisherman, then," said Betty. She helped him up on a chair and handed him the toy fishing pole. She and I went behind a blanket and guided the hook to "catch" a toy. She hooked a bag of marbles.

"Fish on!" she called. "Reel it in."

Mikey reeled but when he saw the marbles, he looked so sad, I told him to cast his line again.

This time, I grabbed his line before Betty could and hooked a harmonica. "Fish on!" I called again. You could've lit a darkened room with his big smile.

He immediately began blowing into it. The "music" sounded like a cross between nails on a chalkboard and a whistling radiator.

He ran off, pleased as punch with his catch. "Thanks a lot," Betty said. But she was smiling.

I wondered what Trixie was doing for Halloween. She and I used to love dressing up, trying to outdo each other every year. I've written her a couple of times but haven't heard back yet. Some people aren't meant to be pen pals, I guess.

Sunday, November 1, 1942

DeeDee —

Cold, cold, cold. Rattlesnakes are crawling in from the desert to get warm. Jim killed one with an old golf club when it crawled out from under their building. At least it didn't get into their room! I saw the rattles when I stopped there this morning. Betty and I walked over to Block 17 to warn Mr. Matsui, so he'll be extra careful when he goes out in the desert. He's been collecting bitterwood for carving. He made Mrs. Matsui a cat, holding up a paw. It's so real, you expect it to meow.

Monday, November 2, 1942

DeeDee —

Mr. Crofton knocked on our front door this morning, waving a piece of paper at Pop. It turns out, he's bought this house! Pop called the landlord and he said it was true. Said Mr. Crofton had made an offer that was too good to pass up.

Mr. Crofton's first action as our new landlord was to evict us. He said we have one week to find someplace new to live.

He was practically cackling with glee when he told us.

I was hoping Pop would say we might as well go back to Seattle.

Instead, he went looking for another place for us to live here.

Tuesday, November 3, 1942

DeeDee —

For the first time since Hank enlisted, I wished I hadn't gotten a letter from him. Then I could hope that the *Enterprise* was still in dock, being repaired.

But the letter that came yesterday—which was mailed a while back—said repairs had been finished and they were underway.

If I hadn't gotten that letter, then I wouldn't be worried about Hank being in the battle that was reported in today's paper. It was near the Santa Cruz Islands, east of the Stewarts in the Pacific. The first couple of paragraphs of the article talked about how "American forces inflicted severe damage on the Japanese fleet."

But farther down were words that made me want to curl up in a ball and hide under my bed: "The loss of an unnamed United States aircraft carrier and the destroyer *Porter* occurred in this engagement."

An unnamed aircraft carrier. A bird boat.

Like the *Enterprise*.

Please, God, don't let it be Hank's ship.

Wednesday, November 4, 1942

DeeDee—

Pop read that the Navy wasn't releasing the name of the destroyed aircraft carrier until relatives had been contacted.

We haven't been contacted yet so he says it's a good sign.

I want Pop to be right about this. I really do.

Thursday, November 5, 1942

DeeDee —

They finished building the watchtowers at the camp today. There are eight of them standing like unfriendly giants. Jim says with hundreds of miles of desert all around us, there's no need for them. Or for all the barbed wire fences.

But they're there.

Friday, November 6, 1942

DeeDee —

Mrs. Sato and Mrs. Tokita and a bunch of the other mothers met with the camp manager today to ask him to do something about the coal situation before their kids all get pneumonia. Betty and Mikey have rotten colds. It makes me sad to see them shivering and miserable without a stove, on top of everything else. I feel guilty, sitting here, writing this, snug and warm in my room.

We've bought up all the blankets in town we could. Miss McCullough is supposed to be arriving tomorrow. Pop's hoping her trunk will be full of blankets.

Saturday, November 7, 1942

DeeDee —

Pop found us another house. No window seat or yellow wallpaper but it's bigger. Last week, we had two college students sleeping in our front room. They'd gotten camp releases so they could start college in Ohio but needed a place to stay until their train left. None of the hotels in town would rent them rooms. Our new house has five bedrooms so Pop says we can run a regular hotel.

And here's the funniest thing: We only have to move kitty-corner across the street. Pop said that made Mr. Crofton spitting mad.

Good!

Sunday, November 8, 1942

DeeDee —

No word from Hank. Pop says "no news is good news."

I pray that's true.

Monday, November 9, 1942

DeeDee —

We got a short letter from John today. He says that girl in his history lecture is Donna Brown and she takes very good notes that he is making a habit of borrowing. Not that he needs to; it's only an excuse to talk to her.

At least *someone* is having fun somewhere.

Tuesday, November 10, 1942

DeeDee —

Heard from Margie. After so many short, quick notes, this was a real letter.

Everything's fine at home. One of the bathroom pipes started leaking but Pastor Thomson helped her fix it. "I'm starting to know my way around the business end of a wrench these days," she wrote. "I did go to the church as you asked, Pop, and found the box Mrs. Harada wanted. I've brought it home and added it to the pile of other boxes you've mentioned. Pastor Thomson plans to drive over your way in the next week or so. If that doesn't work out, he'll look into shipping the boxes by train."

Next she wrote out her recipe for meat loaf. "Please give this to Miss McCullough as she specifically asked for it." I couldn't imagine why — maybe Miss McCullough wanted to poison somebody!

The end of her letter was all about Stan. He's still training in England. From there, he doesn't know for sure where he'll be sent. "He did say the scuttlebutt among the GIs was that they'd be headed to North Africa to take on the German troops there," she wrote. "But his higher-ups are tight-lipped about plans. It's all hearsay, really. At least with Hank, we have a general idea of where he is. Of course, I fret every time I read the news about the fighting in the Pacific because they give so few details. We never know if Hank's in that battle or not. So maybe it will be easier, in a strange way, not to know exactly where Stan is. It really doesn't matter. I'll worry no matter what." I hadn't stopped to think how tough it must be for Margie. She's got a brother *and* a husband in the war. She's a tough cookie, but that's a lot for anyone to handle.

Wednesday, November 11, 1942 —
Armistice Day

DeeDee —

We celebrated the holiday by registering for school. It's kind of funny to even use the word "school." We'll be meeting in one of the barracks in Block 23. Right now, there aren't any desks, just long tables and benches like the ones we sit on in the dining hall. The books haven't arrived and there aren't any blackboards but our teachers say we'll make do.

Even though we're a grade apart, Betty and I have Core class together. After we got signed up, a bunch of the high school kids were goofing around, teasing us junior high "babies." This one kid snatched my binder from me and started to play "keep away." One look from Jim and the kid gave it right back.

It's kind of funny. At Washington Junior, I saw mostly white faces. Here, at the camp school, there are only three of us — me and the principal's sons. It made me feel kind of itchy in my own skin. I wished I could be like a snake and shed it, to look more like everyone else. I wonder if that's what Betty felt like sometimes, back in Seattle.

It's the strangest thing. Back home, I blended in with the crowd. Here, I stand out like a piece of lint on a black dress. Nobody treats me bad or anything but it is a funny feeling.

After getting registered, I walked over to the Matsuis' apartment. Mrs. Matsui was sitting up, having some broth. Mr. Matsui handed me a small package, wrapped in a piece of the funny papers. Inside was a delicate carved wooden bird. "Sandpiper," he said. "For Piper." The legs were as delicate as lace and its head was cocked slightly as if searching for something tasty on the beach. That beautiful thing erased all the strangeness of my day.

It's on my dresser right now, watching over me as I write.

Thursday, November 12, 1942

DeeDee —

We're getting into a routine. This is what a normal day looks like: Pop and I have oatmeal or flapjacks—the two things he can cook—for breakfast. Then we hop in the Blue Box for the drive to Minidoka. Even though we've been doing this for over a month now, the guard asks for Pop's identification every time we come to the gate. After he looks it over and waves us through, we park by the administration building.

Pop goes to the waiting room to see if there's anyone there who needs his help. Then he does visitations, meets with the camp manager, and works on his sermon.

Meanwhile, I head down the road, past the MPs and the hospital to Block 5, to meet up with Betty and Jim to walk to school. I probably walk just as far to Hunt — that's what they've named the school — as I did to Washington from home. Things are spread out here in camp.

Some days, after school, Betty and I go to the canteen for a Coke. She'll walk home with Jim and Yosh, and I stop in to see the Matsuis. Once in a while, I'll walk the other way and stop in to see Mrs. Tokita and Kenji. She's teaching in the nursery school now and usually has some project for her class that I can help her with. Then I meet up with Pop at the administration building around four and we head home for supper with Miss McCullough — who is a much better cook than Margie! I read the paper, do homework, listen to the radio, write letters, and go to bed.

An ordinary day in the ordinary life of the ordinary Piper Davis.

Friday, November 13, 1942

DeeDee —

I went along with Pop tonight when he spoke to the Ladies' Aid Society at the Twin Falls Christian Church. They think, just like Debbie Sue's dad, that the Japanese are getting all sorts of special treatment while the rest of the country has to scrounge to get sugar or coffee.

Pop invited them out to Minidoka, to see for themselves the kind of luxurious life the Japanese are living.

Sunday, November 15, 1942

DeeDee —

I went home with Betty after church. We were setting up the board to play Monopoly when Jim asked if he could play, too.

Betty asked if it was okay. I said sure.

"We'll play by Sato rules," Jim said. I looked at Betty and she looked at me.

"We have special rules?" she asked.

"We do now!" he said.

We picked our pieces. Betty was the top hat and Jim and I squabbled over the race car. Then he gave in and took the purse. He thought that was hysterical.

We rolled to go first. Jim lucked out. "Okay. Rule Number One. You have to sing a song while you count out your move."

"Oh, come on." Betty rolled her eyes.

I turned my finger in a circle next to my head. "He's mad, I tell you," I said to Betty in a fake whisper. "We'd best humor the fellow."

Every few minutes, Jim piped up with a new rule. If you drew a Chance card, you had to create a new dance step. He got Mikey and Tommy in the act, too. Mikey squeaked on his harmonica and Tommy pounded on an empty oatmeal container with a wooden spoon anytime someone passed Go.

By the time he came up with the rule that we had to crow like a rooster if someone landed on one of our properties, Betty and I were laughing so hard, we fell right out of our chairs.

And that made us laugh even harder.

Later, riding home in the Blue Box with Pop,

I broke out laughing every few minutes just thinking about the game. It felt like I'd spent the afternoon with Hank.

There's nothing like a big brother.

Monday, November 16, 1942

DeeDee —

Cold and rainy. I shared my umbrella with Betty and Jim as we walked home from school.

Tuesday, November 17, 1942

DeeDee —

Rain! Rain! Rain! Maybe we should build an ark. Mikey made a little boat out of two pieces of wax paper and a stick and was floating it in a puddle by their stoop this morning. At least he was having fun.

None of the rest of us are, trying to get around. The rain has turned the dust to mud. It's like trying to walk in peanut butter. And with the rubber rationing, lots of people don't have boots or galoshes.

Silly me — I didn't think anything could be worse than the dust.

DeeDee —

I stopped off at the Satos' after leaving Mr. Matsui today. I wanted to show them the squirrel he'd carved. He's already made me a robin and a fox but my favorite piece is still that tiny sandpiper. Betty and her mom were off doing laundry; Jim was there, in charge of the little boys.

"Speaking of your menagerie," he said, as I showed them the squirrel, "I have something for you."

"I helped," said Mikey.

"Me, too," Tommy chimed in.

"But it's not my birthday. Or anything." I couldn't imagine what was up.

"This is a just-because present," said Mikey.

"Just because," Tommy repeated.

The three of them lifted a blanket-wrapped object out from behind one of the beds. Jim carefully pulled the blanket off a small, delicate shelf. It was about one foot long with ends that looked like little scrolls.

I told him it was beautiful.

"It's for your collection," Jim said. "I nailed that

branch there on the front edge to keep the carvings from falling off."

"I love it. But how on earth did you make it?" I held the shelf out, admiring it.

He shrugged. "I used to help Dad in his workshop. Don't get too carried away. A shelf is not that hard to make," he said.

"Thank you. Thank you so much." I carefully set the shelf down and gave Mikey and Tommy a hug. "I'll think of you boys every time I look at this."

I gave Jim a quick hug, too. Then I picked the shelf up again and held it in front of me, admiring it. "Jim, this is the nicest thing anyone's done for me."

"I'm glad you like it." Jim scratched his head. "Really glad."

I hung it up in my room as soon as I got home. It's perfect.

Friday, November 20, 1942

DeeDee —

Jim didn't walk with us this morning. He had to get to school early for something. That was fine with me. It was easier to chitchat with Betty when he wasn't around.

We talked about Thanksgiving coming up, and the letter they'd gotten from their dad. He had written that some of the other men in the camp had been able to leave, to join their families. So he was looking into what he would need to do.

I crossed my fingers and said I hoped it would all work out.

We talked about a few other things and then Betty said, out of the blue, "You know you have a secret admirer, don't you?"

"I do?" My mind went over the boys in my classes. "Well, he's doing a good job of keeping it a secret."

Betty shook her head. "Not that good a job. Not when he makes you a whatnot shelf."

I stopped right there in front of Block 21. "Jim?"

She nodded.

"But he's my friend. My substitute big brother." I thought of the hug I'd given him yesterday. I'd meant it in a friendly way. Nothing like the ones I'd given Bud. What must Jim have thought?

She shrugged. "I guess that's not how he sees it." The rain started up again. "Come on, let's hurry or we'll get soaked."

It's no wonder I flunked the pop quiz in Social

Studies. How could I be expected to name all 48 state capitals after news like that?

I mean, I like Jim. *Like* him.

What a pickle!

Saturday, November 21, 1942

DeeDee —

Mikey's been going over to Mr. Matsui's after school to learn how to carve, too. Today, he gave Mrs. Harada a flower he'd made. It was pretty good for an eight-year-old. She put it in an empty hair tonic bottle and now Mikey says he's going to carve her a whole bouquet.

Sunday, November 22, 1942

DeeDee —

I saw Jim in church today for the first time since Betty's announcement. I felt so awkward around him. Did he know that Betty had told me? Did he think I felt the same way? I was so discombobulated that I spilled a cup of tea on myself after services.

Jim handed me a towel to clean up. "You look a little peaked," he said. "Are you okay?"

"Yes," I said out loud. Inside, I said, *No, no, no.*

Monday, November 23, 1942

DeeDee —

A coal shipment finally arrived! And, even better, when I stopped off at the Satos' this morning, their apartment was warm.

"Isn't it the most beautiful thing you've ever seen?" Mrs. Sato showed off the squat black potbelly stove. I nodded, doing my best to avoid eye contact with Jim. I was so confused about how to act around him. I wished Betty had never said anything.

"I bet you got to scoop in some of the coal," I said to Mikey. He nodded.

"Me, too," said Tommy.

"How'd you guess?" Mikey asked.

"I'm a mind reader," I said. Then I laughed and pointed at their dirty hands.

"Let's get you guys washed up before school." Jim hustled his little brothers out the door.

"School!" Betty said. "I don't even want to go today. This is the first time my innards have been thawed out in two months."

Laughing, we walked, arm in arm, across camp to class.

Tuesday, November 24, 1942
DeeDee —

Big surprise: It rained again. I watched one of the little first-grade girls try to make her way to school. First, she'd reach down and tug on the top edge of one boot to lift her foot out of the muck. Then she'd put that foot down and do the same thing with the other boot. At the rate she was going, she wouldn't make it to school until Christmas! I asked her if she wanted help and she said yes. I carried her piggyback the rest of the way.

Thursday, November 26, 1942
DeeDee —

Thanksgiving Day. Pop says I should make a list of the things I'm thankful for. Here goes:

Hank's safe (as far as we know)
Mrs. Matsui is feeling a little bit better

It's a short list. As far as I can see, there's not much to be thankful for in this place.

Friday, November 27, 1942

DeeDee —

I finally got a letter from Trixie. She said she was so, so, so sorry she hadn't written sooner. She's dance team captain, which is keeping her hopping. She and Eddy broke up and that is fine with her. She has her eye on this new boy from California, anyway. "He's a dreamboat!" Then she said she hated to be the one to break it to me, but Debbie Sue and Bud have been an item since October. It was funny—that news doesn't even make me sad. It seems like some other Piper was Bud's girl, not me.

At the end of the letter, Trixie promised "on her honor"—which was underlined about twelve times—to be better about writing back in the future. She signed her name with huge loopy flowers dotting the *i*'s.

There was a P.S. that said, "I can't wait until you get home."

But I wasn't so sure about that.

Saturday, November 28, 1942

DeeDee —

They showed an old movie in Block 8 this afternoon. A Western. But it was better than nothing!

Afterward, Jim asked if I wanted to take a walk. I looked around for Betty but she had disappeared. Fink.

"Okay," I said. We slipped into our coats and started walking.

"So did the shelf work out okay?"

"Yes. Thanks again. It was swell of you." The notion that Jim had a crush on me made me feel stiff and awkward.

He blew into his hands to warm them. "So, I hear my sister blabbed."

I tried to act innocent. "What do you mean?"

He tugged on the pom-pom on my hat. "Never play poker. You cannot keep a straight face."

"Jim, look." I grabbed his arm so he'd stop walking. "You are a great guy. And I like you a lot —"

"As a big brother." Even behind his glasses, I could see the hurt in his brown eyes.

I nodded. I had been thinking about this ever since Betty spilled the beans. Thinking about how I'd felt about Bud — kind of a silly, lighter-than-air feeling. A feeling I didn't have for Jim.

"Okay then." Jim put his hands in his pockets and we started walking again. After a few steps, he stopped. "Still friends?" he asked.

I squeezed his arm. "Always friends," I answered.

Monday, November 30, 1942

DeeDee —

I still can't believe it. It seemed like Mrs. Matsui was getting stronger, getting better. But they took her to the hospital last night. Pneumonia. She died this morning.

Mr. Matsui hardly knew we were there when Pop and I went to see him. Pop did most of the talking. I sat there, trying not to look at the empty bed. In the back of my mind, it seemed like there was something was different about the room.

It was the walls. They were empty.

"Where is Mt. Rainier?" I asked. "The sunflowers?" I didn't see the happy cat, either.

He didn't answer. After a minute or so, he pointed at the potbelly stove.

Tuesday, December 1, 1942

DeeDee —

Something's wrong. Mr. Matsui went out to gather bitterwood after lunch and he's not back yet.

And it's started to snow.

Wednesday, December 2, 1942

DeeDee —

Still snowing. Mr. Matsui's still gone.

Thursday, December 3, 1942

DeeDee —

They asked for volunteers for a search party. Pop didn't want me to go but Mr. Matsui's my friend. I had to.

Jim and I were in a group together. He'd gone wood collecting with Mr. Matsui before so he thought he knew which way he might have gone.

This is so hard to write.

Jim and I were the ones to find him.

About 2:30 this afternoon. At first, it looked like he was asleep. So peaceful. A pile of bitterwood branches lay next to him. But something about him told me he wasn't asleep. I hung back and Jim bent to see if he was breathing. He asked if I wanted to go for help or should he. Even though I'd never been around a dead person before, I said I'd stay. I covered Mr. Matsui with the blanket I'd been carrying and sat on the frozen ground.

I'd heard Pop preach enough funerals that the 23rd Psalm kept playing in my head: "He maketh me to lie down in green pastures." There was nothing green about the place where Mr. Matsui was lying down, but I recited it out loud anyway. It comforted me to imagine him in a green field, somewhere, walking with his wife, looking for the perfect place to set up his easel.

It wasn't long before Jim was back with the sheriff and some other men. One of them wrapped a blanket around me. I hadn't realized I was shivering until then. Someone else gave me some hot tea to drink while the sheriff looked everything over. He found matches in Mr. Matsui's pocket. "I wonder why he didn't use these to start a fire," the sheriff asked. "Plenty of sagebrush out here to burn. It might not have kept him real warm, but it would've worked as a signal."

I started shivering even harder then. I pulled the blanket around me as tight as I could, but I still couldn't stop.

Jim came over and rested his hand on my shoulder. "You okay?"

I couldn't find my voice to answer. I didn't think I would ever be as sad as I was at that moment, thinking of Mr. Matsui so lonely and heartbroken that he wouldn't even use those matches. You know how people say they can feel their hearts break in two? That is what I felt like today. My heart couldn't hold itself together anymore and tore right apart, the two jagged edges scraping the inside of my chest.

Jim helped me back to the Blue Box. He said my name and when I looked at him in answer, he just shook his head.

Pop made me some more hot tea when I got home, sweetening it with sugar he'd hidden somewhere. He stoked the stove and covered me with every blanket in the house but I couldn't stop shivering.

Friday, December 4, 1942

DeeDee —

I stayed in bed all day. Pop offered to bring Betty for a visit, but I pulled the blanket over my head and didn't answer.

My heart is still in two pieces. If I concentrate on lying very, very still it doesn't hurt so much.

Once, I dozed off and when I woke up, the first thing I saw was the shelf Jim made with my wooden menagerie on it. I thought about Mr. Matsui gathering the bitterwood, inspecting each piece carefully with his sparkling eyes. He told me he read the wood, to find out what animal was hidden within. Then he would reach for his pocketknife and his wrinkled hands would patiently carve each feather or foot or face. One animal took him so many hours but he never seemed to mind.

He'd had so much taken away from him but he gladly gave these perfect creations away.

To me.

I will never, ever forget him.

Saturday, December 5, 1942

DeeDee —

Pop made popcorn and brought the chessboard into my room and we played game after game after game.

I can't ever remember my father spending a whole day with me. I know he had a lot of things to do. Getting ready for church. Getting ready for the memorial. But he spent the day with *me*. It was like being wrapped up in the softest, fluffiest quilt in the world.

I have finally stopped shivering.

Sunday, December 6, 1942

DeeDee —

Pop said I didn't have to but I wanted to go to the memorial for Mr. Matsui. It was in Block 28, in the social hall where we hold church. Pop did the service so I sat with Mrs. Harada. We held hands the whole way through and afterward she gave me a hug, with an extra squeeze. It was her way of telling me she wanted to squeeze the sad out. I wish a hug really could do that.

While the adults gathered in small clumps, Jim came up to me. "Let's get some fresh air." Our breath hung like comic strip bubbles in the cold air as we paced around. We walked by the well, around the high school in Block 23, and past an area where there was talk of building a ball field come spring.

Jim turned me so my back was to the camp buildings. In front of me stretched a patch of frozen ground that went on forever. "I hate this place," I said. "Everything about it is ugly."

"Now it's ugly," Jim said. "But there's beauty out there."

I told him he was nuts. He told me to pretend it was summer. July. August.

I shivered. I didn't think my imagination was that good.

He started talking. About rows of zucchini and carrots and cucumbers and radishes and peas.

"I don't like peas," I said.

"You'll like these. Fresh. Right out of the pod." He kept talking, pointing farther off to where there would be cabbage and potatoes and broccoli and eggplant. And sunflowers.

His words were like Mr. Matsui's paintbrushes, sweeping color and life across the blank, barren canvas of Minidoka. I could see it — see the gardens and could almost taste the harvest.

He put his arm around me in a big-brother hug. "Every time we make something beautiful out of something ugly," he said, "we will keep Mr. Matsui's memory alive."

We stood there, together, puffing clouds of breath, until our feet were numb.

"It's so unfair," I said, finally.

"A lot of life is," he said. "Some of it we can't do a darned thing about. But we can make a difference in some situations. And I think if we can, we should."

Then without a word, we turned together and walked back to Block 28.

And back to life in the camp.

Monday, December 7, 1942

DeeDee —

As if we needed a reminder, our Social Studies teacher made a big deal out of it being the one-year anniversary of Pearl Harbor. She said it was the perfect opportunity to discuss the implications of Japan's aggression. I could hardly believe my ears.

The coal in the classroom's potbelly stove has more feelings than she does. Despite the fact that all of the kids were staring out the windows or at the floor, she forged ahead, trying to start a discussion about whether the relocation of the Japanese was the right thing to do. Red spots popped up on her cheeks and her voice got shrill as she kept pushing for someone to say something. She called on several of the Nisei students by name, but they looked away and wouldn't answer her. What did she expect?

Then she called on me. My stomach rolled around like a tumbleweed. What did she want me to say? Yes, I thought sending nice men like Mr. Harada away was a good idea? Yes, locking up the people I'd grown up with was a reasonable thing to do? Yes, making any human being live in a camp like Minidoka was the way to win a war?

Though there were so many thoughts crashing around in my head, I didn't say any of them out loud. In the end, I shrugged, too, like everyone else had, and studied the top of the picnic table we use for desks. When I looked up, I caught Betty's eye. She nodded.

One small victory in this crummy war.

Thursday, December 10, 1942

DeeDee —

I've got such a nasty cold that Pop told me to stay home from school. That was fine with me. I feel too lousy even to write letters, though I owe one to Hank.

A girl named Jeanne Takahashi is staying with us for a few days. She's on her way to a nursing job in Chicago. She fluffed my pillows, made me cinnamon toast and tea all day, and put cool cloths on my forehead.

I told her she's the best nurse in the world and she smiled and said she hoped they thought so in Chicago because at her last job all they could see was that she was Japanese.

Saturday, December 12, 1942

DeeDee —

The camp manager gave out extra passes so people could go into town to do their Christmas shopping. Pop took a carload in the Blue Box, including Betty. She and I met up and shopped for the perfect presents to give our big brothers. I decided on a nice Parker

51 pen — so Hank can write me more letters! — and Betty bought a Zane Grey book for Jim because he's read everything in the Minidoka library.

We were so happy with our purchases that we decided to celebrate with ice cream sodas. Betty's partial to strawberry sodas but I'm a chocolate girl, through and through. We walked over to Twin Falls Drug, which has the biggest soda fountain in the city. But when we got there, we saw a new sign in their window. NO JAPS.

Betty said it was so cold, who cared about ice cream, but I said, let's go over to the Falls Café. The only sign in *their* window said BLUE PLATE SPECIAL, $1.00. We went in and ordered our sodas.

But neither of us finished our drinks. I guess we'd both lost our taste for something sweet.

Tuesday, December 15, 1942

DeeDee —

Margie called today. Long distance! It must've cost a fortune but it was so good to hear her voice. First she talked to Pop about the house and work and Stan, who's still in England. When I got on with her, we didn't talk about anything important and that was the best part of all. Ten whole minutes of girl stuff.

It was better than a whole case of Sky Bars.

Wednesday, December 16, 1942

DeeDee —

You can only get one glass of milk a day in the dining hall now. That's kind of hard on the little kids.

We finally started our typing unit at school. Because of the shortage of typewriters, the teacher drew an oversized keyboard on a piece of wrapping paper that she stapled to the wall. During class, she tells us which fingers to use to press which letters. Like, "Right pointer finger, type *j* three times. Left pointer finger, type *f* three times." We have to pretend our laps are keyboards.

It's pretty silly.

Thursday, December 17, 1942

DeeDee —

I looked back in my diary to see when the camp manager promised to have the bathrooms working. It was November 1st! Over a month later and we're still using latrines. Which are flooded from all the rain. I try hard not to use them while I'm at school but Betty and the others don't have a choice.

Friday, December 18, 1942

DeeDee —

Pea-soup foggy and cold. It's hard to believe, but the food is getting even worse in the dining halls. They serve fish every Friday, usually a nasty black cod, which tastes even worse than it smells. And it seems like most weeks are starting to have two Fridays in them!

Monday, December 21, 1942

DeeDee —

For the past two weeks, Mikey and Tommy haven't talked about anything else but the Christmas trees that were coming to their elementary school. (They go to Huntville, in Block 10; Stafford Elementary is for the kids in Blocks 21 through 44.) I'd see them in the dining hall and they'd say, "Do you think they'll come today, Piper?" Or I'd pick Betty up to walk to school and they'd ask me.

Well, today was the "big" day, the one the boys

had been waiting for. And what a bust! Nothing but scrawny and pathetic excuses for trees. Some are just branches. The disappointment from the elementary school hung as thick as a winter fog over the camp. I mean, when you're a little kid, is there anything more exciting than a Christmas tree?

I couldn't stand Betty's little brothers' sad, puppy-dog eyes. She and I put our heads together about what to do. The answer was practically right in front of us! Sagebrush. That is *one* thing there is no shortage of here. After school, we wandered around behind Block 29, where the Victory gardens are going to be planted come spring. It took a while but we found a tree-shaped clump of sagebrush and dragged it back to the high school. We "requisitioned" some silver spray paint from the art supply cupboard and went to work. After supper, we snuck the "tree" into the boys' classroom. Mrs. Harada had a supply of red ribbon she'd given to us. Betty tied bits of it around whole walnuts and hung them in the silver. I brought the animals Mr. Matsui had carved for me and set them in the branches.

Betty posed next to our "tree" and I snapped a photo to send to Hank. Then she took my Kodak from me. "You're always behind the camera," she said. "You need to be in front of it once in a while!" Before we turned off the lights to leave, we stood back and admired our creation. I'd give anything to see the boys' faces in the morning!

Pop said during the Great Depression there was this saying: "Use it up, wear it out, make do, or do without." If there is one thing I've learned at Minidoka, it's how to make do.

Betty and I both agreed it was a beautiful tree, no matter what. I thought about Trixie's mom and how every year their tree had a different color scheme. She had some of the fanciest Christmas trees I'd ever seen. But I don't think any of them hold a candle to this one.

Thursday, December 24, 1942

DeeDee —

I want to be back in our own house, on Spruce Street, hanging stockings with Margie and Hank — and Stan, too, of course. And I want to have meatballs and rice pudding with Mr. and Mrs. Harada, like we always do on Christmas Eve, and I want Pop to read the Christmas story.

There's nothing good about Christmas Eve in Twin Falls. None of our family is here. Our stockings are in Seattle. And Pop and I tried to make meatballs and ended up eating fried egg sandwiches.

Ho, ho, ho.

Christmas Day, 1942

DeeDee —

Santa brought a special delivery. Margie! She took the train clear from Seattle to spend the holiday with us. It was a total surprise. Well, Miss McCullough knew about it and had picked her up at the train station. We made fudge and played gin rummy and told Hank stories. Margie even brought presents. She'd sewed bolero vests for me and Betty; mine's green and Betty's is blue. I slipped mine right on over my best white blouse and it fits perfectly! And she brought Pop some Prince Albert tobacco and a pair of fur-lined driving gloves, which he could really use. The Blue Box's steering wheel practically freezes in this cold weather. Miss McCullough roasted a chicken for supper and then afterward we all went to the camp.

There was a decorating competition between

the blocks. I heard Dining Halls 17 and 36 tied for the best decorated, but I thought that Block 5, where the Satos and Mrs. Harada live, should've won. White crepe paper and red paper lanterns were strung from the ceiling and the tables had been waxed until they gleamed. Up front, where the food was served, hung green construction paper letters spelling out MERRY CHRISTMAS. Mrs. Harada had cut them out and each letter was a work of art. Someone's record player blared scratchy versions of Christmas carols.

Jim produced Santa hats. He plunked one on my head and the other on Betty's. "You elves can help Santa," he said. "Come with me." He handed us each a big basket overflowing with cellophane bags of candy. He grabbed a basket loaded with oranges and packets of nuts.

"Ho, ho, ho!" he called out. "Come see what Santa's elves have for you!" Mikey and Tommy were first in line. Every single child got an orange, a packet of nuts, and a bag of candy.

"Here you go," I said to one little girl. She took the bag of candy and carried it back to her mother like it was full of precious jewels. I watched her open the bag and examine each piece of candy. Then she gave one to her mom and one to her dad before she took one for herself.

Tonight, I almost forgot that I was in a camp. I sure hope that was true for Betty and the rest.

Sunday, December 27, 1942

DeeDee —

Margie stayed as long as she could, I know. While she was here, she taught Betty and me a new card game called Spite and Malice, trimmed my hair, and talked Pop into letting me wear my Tangee lipstick to school on Fridays.

Margie is a big band orchestra all by herself, so much fun and energy. When she left this morning, the zing went out of the house. I think Pop even felt it because he kept fiddling with the volume knob on the radio, as if the Andrews Sisters belting out "Boogie Woogie Bugle Boy" could make up for the quiet Margie left behind.

She says she'll try to come back at Easter.

Twin Falls felt like home with my sister here.

Friday, January 1, 1943

DeeDee —

Betty and I were talking about New Year's resolutions and Jim overheard us. He pounded his chest like Tarzan and said he doesn't need to make any because he's perfect. Betty threw her pillow at him.

It's the kind of stuff Hank and I used to do, too. When he was home.

Monday, January 4, 1943

DeeDee —

The mud is finally frozen. It's hard to walk on because it's rutted and slick but it's a lot less messy, that's for sure. The PE class is helping to build a skating rink where the ball fields will be. It should be done in a week or so. I don't have skates but Betty knows someone who will share with us. I can't wait!

Saturday, January 9, 1943

DeeDee —

Riding the wildest roller coaster created would be tame compared to the ups and downs I feel when we hear from Hank. I get so excited when I see one of those envelopes with his chicken scratch on the front. But then I slip into worry about what I'll find inside.

Today's letter was full of the censor's handiwork. One huge chunk was completely cut out! But I did get the gist of it: They'd been seeing a lot of action and he was proud to be part of this crew. "The Navy brass tends to underplay things so when you read in the papers that we beat the Japanese, it's Beat, with a capital *B*. They may have more equipment but we do just fine." I knew from all his years of playing sports that Hank is no braggart. If he says something, it's true. His letter gave me hope.

It's been so long since he and I had used our code that it took me a minute to decipher what he'd written at the end of the letter: "lelt yettb shankt rof lla eht setterl."

When I told her, she blushed.

Exactly what have Betty and Hank been writing to each other? Hmmmm.

Monday, January 11, 1943

DeeDee —

Finally, finally the Navy's talking — in the paper today, the Navy Department reported on the losses in the Battle of Santa Cruz islands. The *Hornet* was eventually sunk but not before its planes helped shoot down 156 Japanese warplanes. And listen to this: "At the height of an attack, a 1,000-pound bomb pierced the *Hornet*'s deck and entered the room next to the ordnance room — and it did not explode. The ordnance chief entered the room and disarmed the bomb — in the dark!" Can you imagine being that calm and cool? I sure can't.

It sounds like it was quite the skirmish — the paper said we dropped over 20,000 pounds of bombs and sunk four of their transport ships. Seems hard to imagine any ship, on either side, surviving that kind of fighting. Maybe Hank's right — no matter what they throw at it, the Japanese navy will never take down the *Enterprise*.

Tuesday, January 12, 1943

DeeDee —

So much for ice-skating — the water they pumped into the rink last night leaked out.

Can it get any colder? Or foggier?

I wrote another long letter to Hank and signed it "Your sister, the Pipersicle."

Thursday, January 14, 1943

DeeDee —

It's eight below but at least the sun is shining. Our teachers make us rotate seats every half hour because when you sit near the potbelly stove, you fry, but when you're sitting across the room from it, you freeze. This game of musical chairs might be funny if we weren't so miserable.

When we got back to Twin Falls at the end of the day, we found a letter from John. We hadn't heard from him in a while so it was good to get caught up. He bragged about his first-quarter grades, writing, "Maybe I really will be Professor Anderson like Piper said!" He says college is growing on him and not just because Donna is in several of his classes, but that it doesn't hurt.

I worry about him — he sounds pretty sweet on this Donna. I wonder how she feels about him?

Sunday, January 17, 1943

DeeDee —

Trixie finally wrote again. She apologized for taking so long to write back, blah, blah, blah. Her letter was full of school news but she must be running with a whole new crowd. I didn't know any of the kids she mentioned.

Seattle feels farther away than ever.

Wednesday, January 20, 1943

DeeDee —

It hit 12 degrees below today. If you don't wear mittens, your hands will stick to the doorknobs! I didn't care how I looked — I wore two coats to school. At least I have two coats.

DeeDee —

The Hazelton Lions Club wives came on a tour. Betty and I got excused from class to escort them around. The ladies were all dressed up with not one pair of galoshes between them.

"How far do we have to walk?" the chairwoman asked.

I pointed up the road to Block 4. "We thought you'd like to see the nursery school and one of the elementary schools, and then we'll walk over to Block 7 for lunch."

We tried to find the driest path, but those pumps they were wearing were no match for the muck. One lady stepped right out of her spectators, landing stocking-footed in the mud. Luckily, Betty had some tissues in her pocket to help clean her up.

The ladies *ooh*ed and *aah*ed over all the cute toddlers in the nursery school. "How wise to simply bring out a few toys at a time for the children," one lady said. The nursery school teacher told her that these were *all* the toys the kids had.

We wandered through the Huntville school in Block 10 — Mikey and Tommy both came running over to say hi when they saw us. Betty made them shake hands with each of the ladies. I heard someone whisper, "They don't have desks. Not even a blackboard." Another lady pressed her lips together and shook her head.

I took a sniff before we entered the dining hall. "You're lucky! It's not a sauerkraut day." Most of the visitors picked at their lunches and I don't blame them. Yuck—fatty roast beef with canned vegetables cooked to mush. I wasn't sure if we'd been served green beans or peas. There was no butter for the rolls, no milk or sugar for the tea.

The ladies were awfully quiet as they left, ruined shoes and all.

I doubt anyone in town will think the Japanese are pampered after this.

Sunday, January 24, 1943

DeeDee—

After services today, that really swell English teacher, Miss Young, talked to a bunch of the kids about starting a glee club. I knew better than to volunteer. I'm so tone-deaf I got asked to leave the church choir in third grade! But Betty signed up and Jim, too.

Tuesday, January 26, 1943

DeeDee —

Pop had a meeting at the camp tonight so I stayed after school to listen to the first choir practice. Miss Young picked four of the boys to be in a Men's Quartet. Jim's one of them.

Betty and I think he has the nicest voice of the whole group.

Thursday, January 28, 1943

DeeDee —

There was a big buzz over at the high school today. At lunchtime, we found out why. The Army has announced that it's organizing an all-volunteer Nisei combat unit. This one kid said he'd never sign up. "Let them fight their own wars," he said. "They don't care about me. I don't care about them." Some of the other guys agreed, but someone else said, "We're American, too. This is our chance to prove it." Boys can get so loud and rough when they argue. I was scared there'd be a fight but it was noise, that's all.

Jim was real quiet during the whole to-do. I wondered how he felt about it, especially with his father in prison. Did he think America should fight its own wars? Or did he think he should join up to prove his loyalty? He isn't a talker so there isn't a way to know. One thing I do know: He's eighteen. Old enough to enlist.

I could tell by Betty's face that she was thinking about the very same thing.

Friday, January 29, 1943

DeeDee —

A bunch of kids put on some records in the social hall after school. Jim and Yosh started a competition for worst dancer, with both of them trying hard to win.

Betty and I hung off to the side, watching the high school kids act completely crazy. Someone grabbed her hand and she was gone, dancing, and before I knew it, I was, too.

When Betty and I crashed together on the dance floor a few turns later, we held one another and laughed so hard we couldn't stand up.

I don't know what made me think about it, but I looked around the room and noticed mine was the only Caucasian face in the crowd.

It was funny. Now I feel more at home than out of place.

Sunday, January 31, 1943

DeeDee —

After church today, Jim cornered Pop. I was too far away to listen in but I did see Betty watching them talk, chewing the fingernails on her right hand.

Jim was probably just asking about his dad.

Nothing for Betty to worry about.

Monday, February 1, 1943

DeeDee —

This time it's for real. No more latrines! I never thought I'd be so excited about a sewage disposal plant! And real toilets. And it only took six months to get them working.

Tuesday, February 2, 1943

DeeDee —

I know an enemy like Admiral Shimada is the last person I should believe, but it's still scary when I read headlines like the one in today's newspaper: JAPANESE CLAIM 5 ALLIED WARSHIPS.

I'm going to paste in part of the article here.

> On Jan. 29 at twilight a great enemy fleet consisting of large numbers of cruisers, battleships and destroyers was sighted west of Rennell Island by our planes, which carried out a surprise attack, sinking by direct hits one battleship and two cruisers while some more warships were damaged.

I looked on the globe. Rennell Island is about 150 miles south of Guadalcanal in the Solomons. And we think that's about where Hank is.

The Office of War Information says that the Japanese reports have all "proved to be false or highly exaggerated." But then they don't say what really happened. I know they can't because "loose lips might sink ships."

I feel like an ant at a picnic sometimes, but instead of waiting for a crumb of pie to fall my way, I'm waiting for a crumb of news—good news—about Hank.

Friday, February 5, 1943

DeeDee —

Here is today's headline: PACIFIC FRAYS GO ON, BUT NAVY WITHHOLDS ALL DETAILS AS POSSIBLE HELP TO ENEMY.

That pretty much says it all.

Saturday, February 6, 1943

DeeDee —

A letter from Hank! Reading it was a bit like reading something out of a time capsule; he had written it before the battle at Rennell Island. But getting it makes me feel like he has to be all right.

He says a couple of the pilots have taken him under their wings — "no pun intended," he wrote. "These guys seem to think I might have what it takes to be a pilot, too. When I watch them release from the deck, I pretend I'm in that cockpit. I figure after maneuvering the old Blue Box around, I ought to be able to handle a fighter plane. Oh, well. It's a nice dream." He signed off with "Hey, sis, I'm feeling kind of homesick. Dens eoms eorm shotop!"

I hadn't taken a picture since Christmas and then it was only because of the tree for Mikey and Tommy. The move and everything had taken too much out of me. I'd lost my love for the camera. But, for Hank, I'd get it back out. I started by taking photos of the Satos and Mrs. Harada, and then I asked Miss McCullough to take one of me and Pop. It felt good to be looking through the viewfinder again.

Sunday, February 7, 1943

DeeDee —

There's a meeting tonight in Dining Hall 3. The Army's sending someone to talk about volunteering for the all-Japanese unit. The 442nd Regimental Combat Team. Jim and Yosh were talking about it after church. "We should at least go," Yosh said. "Hear the guy out."

"No, don't," Betty said, tugging on Jim's arm. "I don't want you to."

Jim gave her a hug. "Sis, going to a meeting doesn't mean I'll sign up."

Betty pushed Jim away. "It better not. We can't take one more thing. Not with Dad gone."

Jim started to say something but Betty interrupted him. "I mean it." Then she looked at me. "Piper, you talk some sense into him."

I had to say something, even though I knew it wouldn't make any difference. Not if Jim had already made up his mind. I put my arm through Betty's. "We've already got one brother between us in the fight," I said. "We don't need two."

"That's right." Betty put her hands on her hips.

Jim bowed low. "I will obey your commands, fair ladies."

But I had a feeling he was only saying that to keep Betty happy.

Monday, February 8, 1943

DeeDee —

If I had known shoes were going to be rationed next, I would've bought a new pair of saddle shoes with my Christmas money!

Good thing my feet haven't grown much lately.

Friday, February 12, 1943

DeeDee —

At lunch break, we could smell the fish from the dining hall from a block away. We didn't even bother going in.

Saturday, February 13, 1943

DeeDee —

Somehow word got around about me and my camera. I was busy all afternoon taking photos of different families. I was especially proud of the one of Mrs. Tokita with little Kenji. Who isn't so little anymore! He says complete sentences. After I took their picture, he said, "Picture for Papa." Mrs. Tokita's eyes welled up and she gave him a hug. "Yes. We will certainly send this picture to Papa."

Little Kenji is growing up so fast. It must be tough on Mr. Tokita not to be here to see that.

Sunday, February 14, 1943

DeeDee —

Margie and Stan's first anniversary. I hope it's their last one apart. We called her to wish her a happy anniversary. She said Stan was still training in England but that he'd heard a rumor they'd need their sea legs soon. I asked her why an Army guy needed sea legs and she just sighed. "I think that means he's going to be shipped somewhere," she said. "But I have no idea where. And even if he knew, he couldn't tell me. It wouldn't get past the censors."

The Men's Quartet sang at church. It was a nice change from Miss McCullough's piano pounding, that's for sure. When they sang, "It Is Well with My Soul," I saw Mrs. Harada dab at her eyes with her handkerchief. I'm sure it's hard for her to feel anything's well with her soul, with Mr. Harada still in Fort Missoula. I gave her an extra big hug when church let out.

Later, the Quartet rehearsed for a performance at a Civic Club meeting in Milner Heights next month. The only song they sang that I didn't like was Glenn Miller's "Wishing." The boys sang it fine;

it wasn't that. But the words were hard to swallow: *"Wishing will make it so; just keep on wishing and care will go."*

If there's one thing I've learned in the past few months, it's that you can wish all you want and it doesn't change one thing.

Wednesday, February 17, 1943

DeeDee —

Pop has been writing even more letters than usual. When I ask what's up, he says it's work. Reports, that sort of thing.

Ministers are very bad liars.

Saturday, February 20, 1943

DeeDee —

The sun was bright and the sky blue today but it was gloomy at the camp.

Pop and I didn't get there until nearly supper-time and that's when we heard the news.

Three hundred Nisei from Minidoka did it. They enlisted.

And one of them was Jim.

Mrs. Sato's eyes were red from crying, but Betty was hopping mad. "He promised me he wouldn't. You were there, Piper. He promised." She slapped the table so hard, her silverware bounced.

I didn't know what to say. "He must think it's pretty important, to break a promise like that."

Betty sniffed. "There's nothing important enough! Nothing."

I got up from the table and brought her back a cup of tea. "Drink this."

She took a few sips. "He thinks it will make a difference in the way we'll be treated. But it won't. It won't."

I thought about that for a minute. "Not that I'm trying to defend Jim or anything—"

"Good," Betty said. "You'd better not."

"But I was just thinking about Dean. You know. The guy from the sugar beet harvest? Working with Jim changed his mind about the Japanese." I shrugged. "I don't know. Maybe having Nisei in the Army will help. Maybe it *will* change things."

Betty stared into her teacup. "Then all I've got to say is that it had better change things. Big time."

I hoped so, too.

Tuesday, February 23, 1943

DeeDee —

I *know* something's up. I get the mail every day and twice now there have been letters from Washington, D.C.

I sure hope Pop's not planning to move *there*.

Friday, February 26, 1943

DeeDee —

The sun was out today for the arrival of the Bainbridge Island Japanese. They'd been at Manzanar but wanted to be here, at Minidoka, with the other Japanese from our state. Mrs. Harada painted a welcome sign that the first graders carried, and a bunch of us hooted and hollered to them as soon as they got inside the gate.

They sure timed it right. The mud's almost all dried up.

Monday, March 1, 1943

DeeDee —

Got a telegram from John — he popped the question and Donna said yes! I think it's swell he found someone to love but I wondered if it would be hard for her, with him missing an arm and all. I asked Pop about it. He said everybody's missing something — a knack for numbers or remembering names or even patience. "John's no different than the rest of us except for the fact that he can't hide what he's missing."

Pop had a point. I mean, look at Mr. Crofton. There was no way to tell by looking at him that he was down a quart in the milk of human kindness.

Wednesday, March 3, 1943

DeeDee —

Pop got a call from the chairwoman of the Milner Heights Civics Club. Her members "object" to a Japanese Quartet singing at their club meeting. Pop told her the Quartet was disbanding anyway, because two of its members had volunteered for the Army.

She didn't have much to say after that.

Friday, March 5, 1943

DeeDee —

Mystery solved about all Pop's letters back and forth to Washington, D.C. He's been trying to volunteer for the Army! And *he* didn't tell me. Miss McCullough accidentally spilled the beans when she came over to fix supper tonight.

"I have to say I'm very thankful the church sees what an important job your father is doing here," she said as she cut up carrots for the stew.

"Was there some kind of problem?" I ate one of the carrot chunks she'd cut.

"No. No. It's just that your father was so persistent —" She stopped in mid-chop, a panicked expression on her face. "He hasn't told you?"

"Told me what?" I said.

She sighed. "I'm so sorry I spoke out of turn. You'd best ask him about it." And that is all I could get out of her.

I pounced on Pop the minute he walked in the door. "Is there something you've been meaning to tell me?"

It all came out. He had volunteered for the 442nd, to serve as their chaplain.

"You mean, you'd leave me here?" I asked. "All alone?"

He shook his head. "I would've sent you home to Margie. That's what you want, isn't it? Anyway, it's water under the bridge because the church higher-ups won't let me go. They think I can do more good here."

Sometimes I think my pop cares more about "doing good" for the Japanese than he does for his own daughter. Sure, I want to go home to Seattle. But not if it means Pop's off in a war somewhere.

Good golly. You'd think my own father could figure that out for himself.

Saturday, March 6, 1943

DeeDee —

It seemed like everyone turned out today to start work on the project farm. Betty and I helped Mrs. Tokita in the kids' Victory garden. Mikey and Tommy looked like someone had tried to plant *them* by the time we were done. I don't know how those two can get so dirty!

At lunchtime, Jim brought Betty and me some tea and the three of us looked out over the camp's big Victory garden, the one the adults were planting. I thought of what Jim had said the day of Mr. Matsui's memorial, when we looked out over the sagebrush-dotted desert.

"It is going to be beautiful," I said.

He knew right away what I was talking about and he smiled and said, "I told you so."

Monday, March 8, 1943

DeeDee —

Miss McCullough is going to stay with me for a few days while Pop goes on a business trip. He's being very mysterious again. Thank goodness, he's got that chaplain stuff out of his system.

Tuesday, March 9, 1943

DeeDee —

I had to promise not to tell Pop, but Miss McCullough taught me how to play poker! We play for bobby pins. I'm losing.

I never knew that Miss McCullough was so much fun.

Thursday, March 11, 1943

DeeDee —

Pop got home late tonight. He looked tired but happy. I'd learned enough from playing poker to guess he had good news.

But he was playing his cards close to his chest.

Friday, March 12, 1943

DeeDee —

In Core class, I whispered to Betty that Pop was acting strange. She said maybe he'd fallen madly in love with Miss McCullough and had decided to propose.

That got us both laughing so hard we got in trouble with the teacher.

Sunday, March 14, 1943

DeeDee —

Margie called. She was feeling lonesome. She hadn't heard from Stan in a while. "I guess that means he's on the move to his next assignment. But it would be good to hear."

I told her about Jim enlisting. She clicked her tongue. "That'll be tough for his mom."

"Do you think it will make things better? Them being in the Army?" I asked.

"Kiddo, if I knew the answer to that, I'd be richer than Midas." Margie sighed into the phone.

"It should, shouldn't it?" I said.

"You've got that right," Margie said. "You've got that right."

Thursday, March 18, 1943

DeeDee —

Miss McCullough and I made cupcakes, which I carried to school in two shoe boxes.

"Have you been shopping?" Betty teased when she saw them.

"Not likely, with the shoe rationing," I answered. It was hard to keep from grinning. Betty would get quite the surprise out of what was in my boxes.

"Smells like vanilla," Jim said as we started off for school.

"Uh." I had to think fast. "I dabbed some behind my ears this morning. Pretend perfume," I said.

"Girls." Jim rolled his eyes.

Just after lunch—hot dogs and sauerkraut again—in Core class, I opened the boxes.

Some of the other kids in the class knew what was up and they joined right in singing "Happy Birthday" to Betty.

The teacher even let me light a candle on Betty's cupcake. "Make a wish," I said.

She blew it out.

"What did you wish?" one kid asked.

Betty got a wistful look on her face. "If I tell, it won't come true."

But I think we all knew what she'd wished for.

Saturday, March 20, 1943

DeeDee—

Pop's secret is no longer secret. I got woken up a bit ago by the Blue Box's headlights in my bedroom window. I've gotten used to people coming and going at the Davis "hotel." Even though Pop and the mystery guests were keeping it pretty quiet, there was something familiar about the voices I was hearing.

I tiptoed to the landing . . .

and burst into tears when I saw who was there, flying down the stairs to throw myself into Mr.

Harada's arms. His face was scratchy from needing a shave but I didn't mind one bit. Then I greeted Mr. Sato and Mr. Tokita.

"How did this happen?" I pulled Mr. Harada to sit on the couch and sat next to him.

"Your father is very persistent," Mr. Sato said.

"And the authorities are coming to their senses," Pop added. "Not one of the men they've taken to Fort Missoula has been found to be guilty of anything."

"Except being Japanese," Mr. Tokita said.

They were quiet for a moment but then I couldn't stand it. "Wait until you see little Kenji. He chatters like a blue jay!" That got them all laughing.

"We're going to make a surprise delivery to camp tomorrow," Pop said. "Be sure to bring your camera."

I said I would. I didn't want to miss these reunions for anything.

Sunday, March 21, 1943

DeeDee —

I had nearly turned inside out with excitement by the time the Blue Box was loaded with its "special deliveries" and we were headed to camp.

We got to church plenty early. Mr. Harada, Mr. Sato, and Mr. Tokita sat on the pews. I don't know how they could sit still. I was so excited I couldn't get settled anywhere. Would it be best to take photos from the back of the room? From the side? I could hardly think straight.

Finally, the wooden door creaked open. As always, Mrs. Harada was one of the first to arrive. She looked first at Pop, then at the three men, throwing her arms open. Mr. Harada moved toward her stiffly, giving me enough time to frame the shot. I think I caught them just as they came together in a warm embrace. I could barely see through my viewfinder, my eyes were so full of tears.

Mrs. Tokita and Kenji stepped in to the church hall next, hand in hand. When she saw her husband she picked Kenji up and ran. Kenji pushed away from his father at first, crying "No man. No man."

Mrs. Harada said, "He'll remember. He will."

When Mikey and Tommy saw Mr. Sato, they were like two little rockets launching into his arms. I've never heard so much laughing and crying.

It was the best church service I've ever been to in my life.

Monday, March 22, 1943

DeeDee —

Betty and Jim stayed home from school today to get caught up with their dad. Jim hasn't told him yet about enlisting. But he'll have to soon.

Saturday, March 27, 1943

DeeDee —

The Satos got a camp pass so Pop and I drove them into Twin Falls. Mr. Sato's coat was worn to threads; that was all he'd had to keep him warm in the bitter Montana cold. After the shopping, we all went to the café — not Mr. Crofton's but the other one — and had hot roast beef sandwiches and lemon meringue pie.

It felt like Christmas.

Maybe better.

Monday, March 29, 1943

DeeDee —

It's a triple whammy of rationing: Now we'll have coupon books for meat, cheese, and butter. Good thing the camp plans to raise pigs and chickens. That will help.

Friday, April 2, 1943

DeeDee —

John called long-distance to speak with Pop. Turns out he wants us to come to Minnesota in June for the wedding. And he wants Pop to do the ceremony. I thought Pop would say he was too busy but he said yes, that we'll swing it somehow.

Who would've thought John's story would have such a fairy-tale ending?

Tuesday, April 6, 1943

DeeDee —

I've taken down the calendar in my bedroom but there's still the one on the wall in our classroom. Now it's only 25 days until Jim leaves.

With every day that passes, Betty gets quieter and quieter.

Saturday, April 10, 1943

DeeDee —

Betty was in a complete funk today. I couldn't cheer her up with a Sky Bar. Not even when I offered her a whole one all for herself!

I knew what it was. Jim and all the other guys who volunteered for the 442nd take their physicals today. The line outside the hospital snaked all the way up to Block 7, practically.

"Hey, have you thought that he might not pass the physical?" I said.

"He's too darned healthy." Betty rested her chin on her hands.

I thought about that. Even when the rest of the families got colds last winter, Jim stayed healthy as a horse. Not even one sniffle. I was thinking so hard, I didn't even realize I was eating the Sky Bar. "Maybe they won't take him because he wears glasses," I said.

Her face brightened for a split second. But just for a second. "Stan wears glasses and the Army took *him*." She grabbed the rest of the candy bar from me and took a big bite. It was the caramel part, the one she hates.

But she was so worried about Jim she didn't even seem to notice.

Monday, April 12, 1943

DeeDee —

We hit the jackpot today! A whole bunch of Hank's letters came at once. Of course, they're all from weeks ago so we don't know how he is this very minute — or where he is! — but reading his words brings comfort all the same. He's still jazzed about learning as much about planes as he can. "I'm saving my pennies to take flying lessons when I get home," he said. I loved reading those words: "when I get home."

He said he'd heard about Jim. He wondered how Betty was taking it.

I wrote back: "How do you think Betty's taking it? He's her big brother."

Friday, April 16, 1943

DeeDee —

I keep pinching myself to make sure I'm not dreaming. But there's the telegram right there on the kitchen table. Hank's coming home!

Okay, it's only for a little while but I'll take what I can get. I don't understand the whole thing but basically the Navy finally figured out how brave and smart my brother is and tapped him to train as a Naval aviator. That means he has to come back to the States to train, which means he gets a visit home! He'll be here in three weeks! I can't wait.

And maybe, just maybe, the war will be over before he's ready to fly.

Saturday, April 17, 1943

DeeDee —

When we walked into the dining hall for lunch today, there were a bunch of guys gathered around the bulletin board in the back. Pretty soon we heard why: The Army had posted the names of the guys who'd passed their physicals.

Betty grabbed my arm. "Come with me," she said. "I can't face looking at that list by myself," she said.

Jim's Math class always gets out late so he hadn't arrived for lunch. I found the sheet with the *S* names on it and ran my shaky finger down the list.

My heart skipped a beat when I didn't see anyone between Sakamoto and Sawaji. "Yahoo!" I called out. "No Sato!"

Betty peered over my shoulder. But I'd been in too much of a hurry. She reached around me and pointed. "His name *is* on the list. There it is."

We stood there for a few moments and then Betty said she didn't feel like eating lunch. "I think I'll go home."

"Are you okay?" I asked her. I was glad I hadn't had the chance to tell her about Hank yet. That might have been more than she could bear.

She bit her lip. I could see tears in her eyes. "I know this is what Jim wanted, but it's too hard. And I can't forget that he promised me he wouldn't go. That's what really hurts."

"He's doing the best he can," I said.

"I wish I felt that way. But I don't." She tugged on her coat and left.

I got my food and sat down. But I'd lost my appetite, too.

Sunday, April 18, 1943

DeeDee —

Betty must have been watching for us. She flagged the Blue Box down after we'd passed the guards at the gate. I slid across the front seat and she hopped in next to me. She asked Pop if he could do some shopping for her in Twin Falls. He said of course and she handed him a list. I leaned against Pop and read it. In Betty's perfect Palmer script were these items: one yard white cotton fabric, red embroidery thread, a ruler, an embroidery hoop, and a packet of needles.

"Looks like a sewing project," Pop said. She ducked her head and nodded. I thought she was being shy — she is around grown-ups. But then I saw that her eyelashes were damp.

Monday, April 19, 1943

DeeDee —

I stopped in to see Mrs. Harada today. Mr. Harada was out playing Go with some old friends. She gave me a big hug. "You still celebrating about Hank?" she asked. She pulled the teakettle off the potbelly stove to make some tea.

"You're celebrating, too," I said. "Using that teapot."

She smiled. "I said I wouldn't use it until Mr. Harada and I were together again. And I didn't."

We sat quietly while the tea brewed. One of the things I like about Mrs. Harada is that it's okay not to say anything when you're with her. She doesn't get all squirmy with quiet like some people do.

When the tea was steeped, she handed me a cup. "One lump or none?" she asked, laughing. With the sugar rationing, sweetening tea was out of the question.

"None," I answered. The tea was hot so I set it down. "I'm worried," I told her. "About Betty. She's pretty mad at Jim. What if she hasn't forgiven him by the time he leaves?" Betty and Jim were like Hank and me — good friends. What if we'd been on bad terms when Hank had shipped out?

Mrs. Harada sipped her tea. "Betty is like that teakettle. She is hot right now and needs to let off steam." She patted my hand. "It will all work out."

"I sure hope so." I glanced at the calendar above Mrs. Harada's desk. "And I hope it's soon."

Tuesday, April 20, 1943

DeeDee —

This morning, I took Betty the packet Pop had picked up for her. After school she invited me to come back to their apartment. Her mother made us some tea. I'm starting to like drinking it without sugar.

Betty opened the packet, spread the fabric out on the table, and cut off a strip twelve inches wide the whole length of the piece. She folded the larger piece in half, stitching it together along the cut edge, then turning it inside out. It sort of looked like a big bandage. Then she took the ruler and marked off rows and rows of dots on the fabric. While she was doing that, her mother snipped and sewed the twelve-inch piece into two ties which they sewed onto the two short sides of the folded fabric.

Betty cut off a piece of the embroidery thread, doubled it through a needle, and rolled the ends into a knot. Then she handed the needle to me. "We're making Jim a *senninbari*, a thousand-person belt," she told me. "To protect him. Will you make the first stitch?"

"I'd be honored." Mrs. Harada had been right. When push came to shove, Betty would be there for

Jim. "You're a good sister," I told her. She just shook her head and handed me the belt.

It took me a couple of tries but I finally made a decent looking French knot. Mrs. Sato hugged me.

After that, Betty carried that belt with her everywhere — to the mess hall, to school, even to the shower rooms. She asked every girl or woman she met to stitch a knot for Jim. Not one person said no. She asked Mrs. Harada to make the last knot.

A thousand hands touched that *senninbari* for Jim. He would be held in a thousand hearts while he was gone, he would be in thousands of prayers.

I hoped that was enough to keep him safe.

Wednesday, April 21, 1943

DeeDee —

I'm sitting here on the bed looking over at the shelf Jim made me — with Mikey and Tommy's help, of course.

It was nice of Betty to ask me to do a stitch in the *senninbari*, but I wish there was something I could give Jim, too. Something just from me.

But I have no idea what that would be. And time is running out.

Thursday, April 22, 1943

DeeDee —

Sometimes the answer to a question stares you right in the face but you still don't see it. I've been making myself crazy thinking of the perfect farewell gift for Jim and I finally got an idea, thanks to a letter from John.

He'd tucked in a photo of his family — including his fiancée! I was so happy for him and ran to show Pop the photo when it hit me.

That's what I could give Jim!

Friday, April 23, 1943

DeeDee —

I felt like a spy on a dangerous assignment as I skulked around camp today, camera in hand. I managed to get photos of everyone on my list *and* avoided running into Jim! That was a major accomplishment.

Saturday, April 24, 1943

DeeDee —

It cost me extra for the rush developing but it was worth it. Maybe Margaret Bourke-White would've done a better job, but I was proud of this batch. There were Mikey and Tommy, on their knees in the dirt, shooting marbles, with Mr. Harada nearby on an overturned apple crate, watching. I caught Mr. Sato, getting ready to take a sip of his tea; when he saw that, I hoped Jim would feel like he was right there, on the other side of the table from his dad. I got the other three members of the Quartet, his baseball buddies, and Yosh. I even managed to get a picture of his sugar beet harvest pal, Dean. My favorite photo, though, was the one of Betty with their mom. They'd been working in their Victory garden, and Betty popped open a couple of Nehi sodas. She'd just given one to her mom and they clinked the bottles together, in a toast. For some reason, they both started laughing, holding on to each other in sheer joy at the sweetness of the soda or the moment or both. That was the moment I caught them in. The moment Jim could carry with him to the war.

Sunday, April 25, 1943 — Easter

DeeDee —

Maybe I'm growing up, after all. For the first time in my whole life, I listened to one of Pop's sermons from beginning to end. He talked about how things looked pretty grim for the disciples on Good Friday. Their leader had been killed and they were hiding and afraid. What they didn't know — because they were too close to everything — is that good things were coming. "It was Friday, but Sunday was coming," Pop said. Sunday — the day of glory and triumph for Jesus and all his followers. Pop repeated it, "It was Friday, but Sunday was coming!" Some people said it along with him. He smiled.

Then he said there are times in our lives when we are living in the Fridays — "when we are betrayed and beaten down." He slapped the pulpit. "Like the Friday when our Savior was crucified." In times like that, he said, it seems impossible that any kind of good thing, any kind of "Sunday" would be coming. "But you must believe that Sunday *is* coming. Not just this Sunday, Easter Sunday, when we celebrate the resurrection — though that is truly something to celebrate — but the kind of Sunday where men and women are genuinely regarded as equal, no matter where their fathers were born, no matter what the tint of their complexion. That kind of Sunday might not be three days away or three years away or even three hundred years," he said. "But it will come. We must believe that it will come."

He nodded and Miss McCullough pounded her way through "Joyful, Joyful, We Adore Thee" on the rickety piano while the rest of the congregation sang along.

Me, I sat there, finally beginning to understand Jim's decision. He was living in a Friday—mistaken for the enemy, sent away to a camp—but he was choosing to live as if Sunday was coming, as if his actions could change people's ideas and feelings.

I realized how lucky I was to have someone that courageous for a friend.

Monday, April 26, 1943

DeeDee —

When I stopped to pick Betty up for the walk to school, Jim was ready to go, too. I thought for sure he'd skip this last week.

But there he was, carting his textbooks like

everything was normal. Like he wasn't leaving for boot camp in six days.

Later, I figured out he did it because he knew Betty needed him there.

That's the kind of guy he is. The Army is lucky to get him.

Tuesday, April 27, 1943

DeeDee —

One of our Language Arts vocabulary words was "bittersweet." I now know what that really means.

Fifteen days until Hank comes home.

But only five until Jim leaves.

Thursday, April 29, 1943

DeeDee —

Betty wants to plan a tea party for Hank when he comes. She says she needs something to look forward to. Her mom has stashed away a little sugar and they are going to bake Mrs. Harada's oatmeal molasses cookies, Hank's favorites.

Thirteen more days in the good column.

Three more days in the bad.

Friday, April 30, 1943

DeeDee —

Jim got it into his head that we needed to play a base-ball game. So we went out to the field—Jim, Yosh, Betty, me, and the little Sato boys. Pretty soon, there were people of all ages, hitting and running and catching. Mrs. Harada even took a turn at bat. We shouted and laughed and played until it got too dark to see the ball.

Then slowly, like we were each carrying some incredibly heavy burden, we all went back to our homes to wait for morning.

Saturday, May 1, 1943 — May Day

DeeDee —

When I was little, I remember making construction paper baskets—a cone with a stapled-on strap—filling them with flowers, and hanging them on neighbors' front doors. The game was to ring the bell and run away so the neighbors wouldn't know who the flowers were from. Kind of childish, but May Day has always been one of my favorite holidays.

Not this May Day. Today Jim and three others

from the camp left for basic training at Camp Shelby in Mississippi.

The boys marched to the dining hall where the cooks had prepared a special breakfast. Not a Vienna sausage in sight! After we ate, there were so many people crowded around, I could hardly make my way over to say good-bye. Little Mikey was glued to Jim's left leg, and Tommy to his right. Mrs. Sato hovered nearby. Mr. Sato sat at the end of the table, smoking cigarette after cigarette, staring off into space. I got them all on camera.

When I finally found myself next to Jim, I didn't know quite what to say. I gave him the wrapped-up album and told him not to open it until he was on his way. Until he needed a bit of home. He touched the package to his heart. "Thank you, Piper. Thank you." His voice got husky and thick and I wondered if he was going to cry. To lighten things up, I told him not to take any wooden nickels. He smiled and said he wouldn't.

"Promise you'll be careful?" I said. "You don't have to win the war by yourself." I'd said it in a teasing tone, but Jim's eyes darkened as if a storm cloud had passed over.

"I'm no hero," he said. "It'll be easier fighting the

war over there than it will be for these guys"—he ruffled Tommy's hair—"to fight the one here."

I said I'd write him and he said he'd like that. I had promised myself not to blubber, but I did. "I wish you weren't going," I said, tears streaming down my face.

He handed me a napkin. "Me, too."

Betty and I stood arm in arm as Jim and the other boys tossed their newly issued Army duffel bags over their shoulders and headed for the waiting jeeps.

Betty swiped at a tear. "He's leaving. Hurry!"

I held up my camera and began snapping. I couldn't help but think that here I was, taking photos of her brother leaving, while in a week I'd be taking pictures of my brother coming home. My mind had been buzzing with all the plans I had for Hank's short visit—there'd be photos to take of chocolate sodas at the Falls Café, fishing in the canal, Monopoly games with Betty, feasting on Miss McCullough's buttermilk fried chicken, and quiet nights at home. I could hardly wait.

Betty nudged me out of my daydream. I looked at her sweet face, her brown eyes holding back the worry.

Yes, I had a lot to look forward to.

But Betty and Jim didn't have any more time. All they had was today. And I didn't want to miss one shot. I clicked away, imagining us, years and years from now, when we were old ladies, sitting together with cups of tea and talking about this day. Talking about our brave, brave brothers.

The last picture I snapped framed the jeeps, kicking up clouds of dust as they passed through the gate in the barbed wire fence. I managed to catch Jim, standing up in the jeep, waving his hat at us, as he left Minidoka far behind.

I dropped the camera to my side, waving until my arm ached. I waved until Jim and the jeeps were specks on the Idaho desert.

Then I took my friend's arm and we started walking back into the camp. She talked the whole way about the welcome home party for Hank but I know that was to keep from thinking about Jim's going away.

It's funny. A year ago, I wouldn't have known that about Betty. I've learned a lot of stuff since I wrote on the first page of this diary. Mrs. Harada taught me that a good broom and good faith are essential tools when facing the dust of life. Mr.

Matsui taught me that there is beauty to be found, even in the middle of a desert.

But it was Pop who helped me learn the most important thing of all. He made me realize that even if we can't do much about the fences that get built around people, when fences get built *between* people, it's our job to tear them down.

Signing off—

Piper Davis

Epilogue

In 1945, when the last incarceree left Minidoka, Piper Davis returned with her father to Seattle to finish high school. After graduation, she entered the University of Washington to pursue a degree in journalism. She carried her camera with her everywhere and one spring day while photographing the cherry trees in full bloom on campus, she met an artist named Seth Brown. After a whirlwind romance, they were married in their senior year. Following college, Piper went to work for the *Seattle Post-Intelligencer*, where she spent her career as a photojournalist. She won a Pulitzer Prize in 1967 for a photo-essay called "Moving Toward Hope: Migrant Workers in Eastern Washington." She retired from the paper in 2003 but she says she will never retire from taking pictures.

Hank Davis completed aviation training, but after the war, came home to Seattle and went to college on the GI Bill. He married Betty Sato and had a successful career in sales before deciding to follow in his father's footsteps. He is now a visitation pastor at the Seattle Japanese Baptist Church. Betty stayed home to raise their three children, remaining active in the Japanese community. When she was in her fifties, she wrote a memoir about her Minidoka experiences, with her lifelong friend and sister-in-law, Piper Davis Brown.

Pastor Davis returned to the Japanese Baptist Church after Minidoka closed its doors, serving the congregation until 1979. He was honored at a banquet upon his retirement that nearly one thousand people attended.

Jim Sato, like so many members of the valiant 442nd "Go for Broke" Regimental Combat Team, died in France in October of 1944 during an attempt to rescue the Lost Battalion. He was nineteen years old.

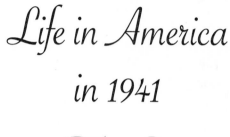

Life in America
in 1941

Historical Note

The 1930s were difficult for America, beginning with the Great Depression in 1929. Thirteen million people lost their jobs, two million people went homeless, and countless others went to bed hungry every night. This time period saw the creation of Hoovervilles, shantytowns for the poor that were named after President Herbert Hoover, on whom many blamed the nation's troubles. When Franklin Delano Roosevelt—FDR—was elected president in 1932, he quickly put his "New Deal" in place, starting the American economy on a slow path to recovery.

In 1939, Germany invaded Poland, launching both World War II and a wartime industry in America, boosting our economy further. Once we entered the war in 1941, over ten million men were drafted into the United States Army (there were eleven to sixteen million men and women in all branches of the service), and women began to be accepted into the workplace to do their part for America. There were many, many "Rosie the

Riveters," like Margie, who performed vital tasks to keep this country and its industries running.

Like other immigrants, Japanese people — 90 percent of whom settled in California — came to America in the early twentieth century looking for opportunities not found in their home countries. Racism and competition for jobs — both of which increased during the Depression — fueled existing anti-Japanese sentiment, leading California (and other states) to pass laws preventing those born in Japan (Issei) from owning land or becoming U.S. citizens. By 1940, there were approximately 127,000 Americans of Japanese descent, or *Nikkei*, living on the West Coast, 80,000 of whom were not only second-generation immigrants (Nisei), but also American citizens.

The attack on Pearl Harbor by the Japanese army on December 7, 1941, was devastating. Over 2,500 people, including civilians like two-year-old Shirley Hirasaki, were killed. Most of the military deaths were men lost on the USS *Arizona*. Delbert and John Anderson are real people and were the only set of twins on the *Arizona* at the time of the attack; John survived and Del did not.

Piper's frustration with getting information

reflects what actually happened. News "blackouts" were ordered in the name of national security. It was days before Americans knew the extent of the damage at Pearl Harbor. However, the headlines on December 8, 1941, made one thing very clear: The United States was now at war with Japan.

The long-standing prejudice against the *Nikkei* intensified and the media quickly painted them as potential spies and saboteurs. President Roosevelt issued Executive Order 9066 on February 19, 1942, which authorized armed forces' commanders to declare any area of the United States as a military area and to "exclude" anyone from that area, particularly people of Japanese ancestry. Beginning in March 1942, 120,000 *Nikkei* on the Pacific Coast were ordered to report to military holding centers, leaving behind homes, jobs, and businesses, even though two-thirds of them, like Jim and Betty Sato, were American citizens by birth.

The Wartime Civil Control Administration set up six stations in Seattle and one in Tacoma to register Japanese families living in the Puget Sound region, provide medical screenings, and "help" them arrange for the sale or storage of their belongings, though there isn't much evidence of that kind of help actually being given. The families were also assigned five-digit identification numbers. Every person in the family was given a tag with the family number on it.

In Washington state, 7,390 *Nikkei* were sent to the Puyallup Assembly Center in early May of 1942. The assembly center, a hastily converted fairgrounds, was nicknamed "Camp Harmony" by an Army public-relations officer. Because the camp was only a temporary "residence," the *Nikkei* were provided few services and fewer comforts. When the first incarcerees arrived, refrigerators and other safe food storage equipment had not been installed yet, and they were forced to eat Army rations. Mattresses were straw-stuffed cotton sacks. Some incarcerees were housed in recently vacated animal stalls. Those in the barracks had no personal space, often using blankets to separate one family's room from another. The slapdash, low-quality construction of the camp offered little protection from the sounds of so many people in tight quarters, making it hard to get a good night's sleep. And, except for sleeping areas, all other facilities were communal. Imagine having to sit on a splintery wooden toilet seat right next to someone you don't even know.

One woman who went to the camp as a fifteen-year-old said she remembered "the shock of seeing the bathroom. It was just holes cut in a plank and there were no stalls. And, no, you had no privacy in the open shower. We were going through puberty and very embarrassed. So we went late at night when no one was there."

The camp itself was surrounded by barbed wire, spotlights, and armed guards. Despite the poor living conditions, incarcerees pulled together, organizing and participating in a variety of activities — like boxing, sumo, softball, knitting clubs, and playing board games like Go and Shogi — to counteract boredom and depression. The younger set even held dances. But Japanese-language books and music were banned. The *Nikkei* developed a self-governing body (eventually replaced with a stricter system overseen by the military), which helped arrange camp jobs for the residents. At Camp Harmony, working forty hours a week, a dishwasher could earn $8 a month, a nurse $12 per month, and a teacher $16 per month. With so many workers gone off to war, some industries, especially agriculture, looked to incarcerees as a source of labor. In total there were about 1,600 volunteers working the sugar beet fields in the American West, including 72 from Camp Harmony who were sent to eastern Oregon and Montana.

The incarcerees were prohibited from using the telephone, so the only access they had to the outside world was through AM radio, subscriptions to English language newspapers, and letters (which were censored). Caring individuals, like Pastor Emery "Andy" Andrews (upon whom Piper's father is based), visited as often as they could, bringing news and supplies. Incarcerees also wrote and printed their own newspaper, called the *Camp Harmony Newsletter*, also censored. It reported on activities and events including sports scores for the camp's teams. Bainbridge Island newspaper owners Walt and Millie Woodward hired several young men (and later, a young woman) to serve as on-site reporters.

Between June and October 1942, the *Nikkei* were moved from the assembly camps to relocation centers in Arizona, Colorado, Wyoming, Arkansas, Utah, California, and Idaho. Camp Harmony residents were moved to Minidoka War Relocation Center in Eden, Idaho. Because so many railcars were in use by the United States Army, the WRA had to recommission ancient passenger cars to transport the incarcerees to the relocation centers. These cars were dirty, had poor water pressure, bad air conditioning, and sealed windows.

The letters and journal entries I read, and the oral histories I listened to, all said the same thing: Minidoka was horrible. Not only did the wicked wind blow volcanic ash dust into everything (even the unappetizing food), for the first several months it had no running water or sewage system. Minidoka was on 33,000 acres of desert, housing about 10,000 *Nikkei* from Washington, Oregon, and Alaska, including 50 people who were part Native American (Eskimo or Aleut). (The camp manager called them all *colonists*, but Japanese Americans now prefer the term *incarcerees*.) It had administration and warehouse buildings, thirty-six residential blocks, schools, fire stations, shops, stores, and a cemetery.

Each residential block had twelve barracks-style buildings, which were divided into six small one-room apartments, a communal dining hall, a laundry facility, communal showers and toilets, and a recreational hall. The families were given Army cots to sleep on and a potbelly stove to heat with. Like the Satos, many families waited months for stoves and the entire camp suffered from a coal shortage through the early months of the first winter (when it dipped to 21 degrees below zero). Rooms were lit by a single hanging lightbulb. The "colonists" were not provided with any furniture, and instead had to fashion it themselves out of scrap lumber. Coal and water had to be hand carried to their apartments, and when coal was scarce they gathered and burned sagebrush to keep warm.

While the relocation centers were subject to the same wartime rationing as the rest of the country, Minidoka developed into a sort of self-sustaining community, with vegetable gardens and chicken and hog farms. Just as they had at Camp Harmony, the "colonists" of Minidoka organized various sports and recreational activities to pass the time, including building a baseball diamond and several parks inside the relocation center. They also participated in Taiko drumming and other musical groups. *The Minidoka Irrigator* was a *Nikkei*-produced newsletter detailing community events, including the performances of the Male Japanese Quartet, and warnings to romantic couples to stop using certain areas for their "lover's lanes."

In January 1943, in need of more manpower, federal officials reversed their decision prohibiting Nisei in the military and announced that they would be allowed to volunteer, even those in the camps. In February 1943, the U.S. War Department and the War Relocation Authority devised a plan to test the loyalty of anyone of Japanese descent over the age of seventeen. The loyalty questionnaires caused much anguish for the incarcerees. Some were bitter about being asked to pledge loyalty to a country that had imprisoned them. The Issei were confused by the questionnaire, which asked them if they would reject their ties to Japan. Doing so would mean they weren't citizens of any country, since they were prohibited by law from becoming American citizens. Despite being held against their will, most Japanese Americans remained loyal to the United States. Some, like Jim Sato, even volunteered for military service. One thousand men and women volunteered from Minidoka, alone—almost 10 percent of the camp's population. That was the largest number of volunteers from any single camp. The 100th Infantry Battalion, and the 442nd Regimental Combat Team—both all-Nisei units—were among the most highly decorated in WWII.

In December of 1944, the Supreme Court ruled that the detainment of loyal United States citizens was unconstitutional, and by January of the following year the detainees were each given $25 and released from camp. Many did not return to the West Coast. Those who did often found their homes and businesses in shambles, despite the promises of neighbors or others to "look after things." None of the *Nikkei* incarcerated in the camps were ever accused of or charged with being a spy or saboteur.

This event was the largest forced relocation in United States history, and while it has been described as the worst violation of constitutional rights in United States history, few Americans were overtly critical of it. Those who did speak out were often ostracized and threatened. It wasn't until the Civil Liberties Act in 1988 that the injustice of the evacuation, relocation, and incarceration of American citizens and permanent resident aliens was acknowledged by the Unites States government. A formal apology was made and restitution was provided to everyone who was interned. In addition, a public education fund was implemented to inform the public of the injustices carried out against Americans of Japanese ancestry, in an attempt to prevent anything of this nature from happening again.

Some helpful websites to learn more about the Japanese internment:

Camp Harmony:
http://www.historylink.org/
http://www.lib.washington.edu/exhibits/harmony/

Minidoka:
http://www.nps.gov/archive/

Incarcerees' Oral Histories:
http://www.densho.org

On the morning of December 7, 1941, the U.S. naval base and Hickam Air Force Base at Pearl Harbor, Hawaii, were attacked by Japanese fighter planes. As a result of the surprise attack, over 2,500 people were killed; more than 1,200 were wounded; and four U.S. Navy battleships were sunk.

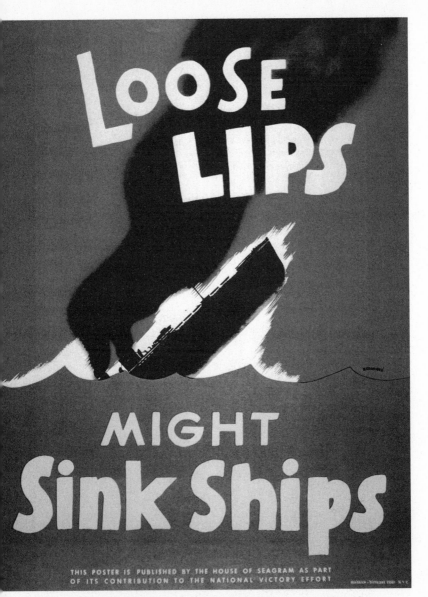

American soldiers were warned not to include details of their whereabouts in letters home.

During World War II, Americans were called upon to plant Victory gardens, as the government rationed foods like butter, sugar, milk, eggs, cheese, coffee, and meat. Produce was also hard to find, with labor and transportation shortages, due to the war effort. At right, a government promotional poster encourages Americans to plant their own gardens. Below, citizens work in their garden in the middle of their suburban neighborhood.

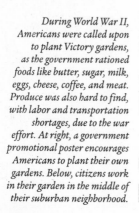

After President Roosevelt signed Executive Order 9066, the U. S. military was able to designate "military areas" at will, which amounted to exclusion zones from which citizens could be rounded up and forcibly removed. Above, an American soldier and Nisei post the Civilian Exclusion Order No. 1 on Bainbridge Island, outside of Seattle, Washington, which gave alien and non-alien persons of Japanese descent one week to leave Bainbridge Island.

3 mile Radius Travel- Dawn to Dusk Curfew For others Permits You had to go to Seattle

WESTERN DEFENSE COMMAND AND FOURTH ARMY
WARTIME CIVIL CONTROL ADMINISTRATION
Presidio of San Francisco, California
April 24, 1942

INSTRUCTIONS
TO ALL PERSONS OF
JAPANESE
ANCESTRY

Living in the Following Area:

All that portion of the City of Seattle, State of Washington, lying generally south of an east-west line beginning at the point at which Judson River meets Elliott Bay; thence easterly along Judson Street to Fifth Avenue; thence northerly to Fifth Avenue to Dearborn Street; thence easterly on Dearborn Street to Twenty-third Avenue; thence northerly on Twenty-third Avenue to Yesler Way; thence easterly on Yesler Way to Lake Washington.

Pursuant to the provisions of Civilian Exclusion Order No. 115, this Headquarters, dated April 24, 1942, all persons of Japanese ancestry, both alien and non-alien, will be evacuated from the above area by 12 o'clock noon, P. W. T., Friday, May 1, 1942.

No Japanese person living in the above area will be permitted to change residence after 12 o'clock noon, P. W. T., Friday, April 24, 1942, without obtaining special permission from the representative of the Commanding General, Northwestern Sector, at the Civil Control Station located at:

1319 Rainier Avenue, Seattle, Washington.

Such permits will only be granted for the purpose of uniting members of a family, or in case of grave emergency.

The Civil Control Station is equipped to assist the Japanese population affected by this evacuation in the following ways:

1. Give advice and instructions on the evacuation.

2. Provide services with respect to the management, leasing, sale, storage or other disposition of most kinds of property, such as real estate, business and professional equipment, household goods, boats, automobiles and livestock.

3. Provide temporary residence elsewhere for all Japanese in family groups.

4. Transport persons and a limited amount of clothing and equipment to their new residence.

The Following Instructions Must Be Observed:

1. A responsible member of each family, preferably the head of the family, or the person in whose name most of the property is held, and each individual living alone, will report to the Civil Control Station to receive further instructions. This must be done between 8:00 A. M. and 5:00 P. M. on Saturday, April 25, 1942, or between 8:00 A. M. and 5:00 P. M. on Sunday, April 26, 1942.

2. Evacuees must carry with them on departure for the Assembly Center, the following property:

(a) Bedding and linens (no mattress) for each member of the family;
(b) Toilet articles for each member of the family;
(c) Extra clothing for each member of the family;
(d) Sufficient knives, forks, spoons, plates, bowls and cups for each member of the family;
(e) Essential personal effects for each member of the family.

All items carried will be securely packaged, tied and plainly marked with the name of the owner and numbered in accordance with instructions obtained at the Civil Control Station.

The size and number of packages is limited to that which can be carried by the individual or family group.

3. No pets of any kind will be permitted.

4. The United States Government through its agencies will provide for the storage at the sole risk of the owner of the more substantial household items, such as iceboxes, washing machines, pianos and other heavy furniture. Cooking utensils and other small items will be accepted for storage if crated, packed and plainly marked with the name and address of the owner. Only one name and address will be used by a given family.

5. Each family, and individual living alone, will be furnished transportation to the Assembly Center or will be authorized to travel by private automobile in a supervised group. All instructions pertaining to the movement will be obtained at the Civil Control Station.

Go to the Civil Control Station between the hours of 8:00 A. M. and 5:00 P. M., Saturday, April 25, 1942, or between the hours of 8:00 A. M. and 5:00 P. M., Sunday, April 26, 1942, to receive further instructions.

J. L. DeWITT
Lieutenant General, U. S. Army
Commanding

Japantown in Seattle, Washington, is closed and boarded up after residents were forced to leave and move to incarceration camps.

Letters sent by Japanese incarcerees at the Department of Justice's Fort Missoula Internment Camp, who were considered "detained alien enemies," were opened and inspected by the U.S. government.

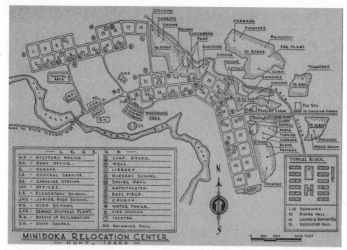

A hand-drawn map of Minidoka Relocation Center, drawn by one of the residents, Anky Arai.

An overview of the Minidoka incarceration camp, in Minidoka, Idaho, showing the long buildings where incarcerees were housed.

The pathways were muddy in Minidoka Relocation Center, making the going difficult, no matter the season.

The inside of a barrack apartment at the Puyallup Assembly Center, in Washington.

Incarcerees at Minidoka decorate one of the dining halls for Christmas.

At Minidoka Relocation Center, incarcerees check the honor roll that lists all of the Japanese Americans from the camp who volunteered for military service. Minidoka had the highest number of volunteers from mainland America.

Piper's dad, Pastor Davis, was based on a real man named Pastor Emery Andrews, who also served the Japanese Baptist Church. When his congregation was interned (mostly to the Minidoka camp in Idaho), he moved his family to Twin Falls to continue to support and care for them. He drove a van called the "Blue Box," in which he made 56 round-trips during war years — even with gasoline rationing — between Seattle and Minidoka, doing errands for the incarcerees.

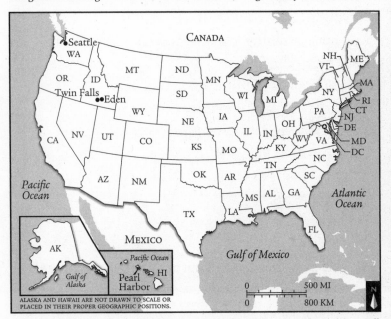

A map of the United States, showing the locations of Seattle, Washington; Eden and Twin Falls, Idaho; and Pearl Harbor in Hawaii.

WWII Oatmeal
Molasses Cookies

INGREDIENTS:

2 cups all-purpose flour

2 cups oatmeal

1 teaspoon baking soda

1 teaspoon baking powder

1 teaspoon salt

1 cup sugar

¾ cup shortening (can use butter)

2 eggs, beaten

5 tablespoons light molasses

2 teaspoons vanilla extract

½ cup chopped walnuts (optional)

½ cup raisins (optional)

DIRECTIONS:

Preheat oven to 350 degrees.

1. In a large bowl, stir together the flour, oatmeal, baking soda, baking powder, and salt.

2. In another large bowl, beat the sugar with the shortening until smooth and creamy; mix in beaten eggs, molasses, and vanilla. Gradually mix in the dry ingredients. Stir in walnuts and raisins, if desired. Drop by teaspoonfuls onto ungreased baking sheets.

3. Bake for 10–12 minutes, or until slightly browned. Allow cookies to cool on baking sheet for 5 minutes before removing to a wire rack to cool completely.

FRANKLIN D. ROOSEVELT'S
Speech to the U.S. Congress
on December 8, 1941 (as delivered)

To the Congress of the United States:

Yesterday, December 7, 1941 — a date which will live in infamy — the United States of America was suddenly and deliberately attacked by naval and air forces of the Empire of Japan.

The United States was at peace with that nation, and, at the solicitation of Japan, was still in conversation with the government and its emperor looking toward the maintenance of peace in the Pacific.

Indeed, one hour after Japanese air squadrons had commenced bombing on Oahu, the Japanese ambassador to the United States and his colleague delivered to the Secretary of State a formal reply to a recent American message. While this reply stated that it seemed useless to continue the existing diplomatic negotiations, it contained no threat or hint of war or of armed attack.

It will be recorded that the distance of Hawaii from Japan makes it obvious that the attack was deliberately planned many days or even weeks ago.

During the intervening time, the Japanese government has deliberately sought to deceive the United States by false statements and expressions of hope for continued peace.

The attack yesterday on the Hawaiian Islands has caused severe damage to American naval and military forces. Very many American lives have been lost. In addition, American ships have been reported torpedoed on the high seas between San Francisco and Honolulu.

Yesterday, the Japanese government also launched an attack against Malaya.

Last night, Japanese forces attacked Hong Kong.

Last night, Japanese forces attacked Guam.

Last night, Japanese forces attacked the Philippine Islands.

Last night, the Japanese attacked Wake Island.

This morning, the Japanese attacked Midway Island.

Japan has, therefore, undertaken a surprise offensive extending throughout the Pacific area. The facts of yesterday speak for themselves. The people of the United States have already formed their opinions and well understand the implications to the very life and safety of our nation.

As commander in chief of the Army and Navy, I have directed that all measures be taken for our defense.

Always will we remember the character of the onslaught against us.

No matter how long it may take us to overcome this premeditated invasion, the American people in their righteous might will win through to absolute victory.

I believe that I interpret the will of the Congress and of the people when I assert that we will not only defend ourselves to the uttermost, but will make very certain that this form of treachery shall never endanger us again.

Hostilities exist. There is no blinking at the fact that our people, our territory and our interests are in grave danger.

With confidence in our armed forces — with the unbounding determination of our people — we will gain the inevitable triumph — so help us God.

I ask that the Congress declare that since the unprovoked and dastardly attack by Japan on Sunday, December 7, a state of war has existed between the United States and the Japanese empire.

From the Author

There are hundreds of stories to be told from World War II — why did I choose this one?

A few years ago, I wrote *Hattie Big Sky*, which is set during World War I, before Piper's story takes place. While I was researching that book, I came across an interview with a German American woman who, the day after Pearl Harbor, brought two sacks of groceries to her Japanese American neighbors. "I remember during the other war," she told them, "when my mother couldn't buy any food anywhere. I am afraid that might happen to you." This interview brought tears to my eyes. Just think — over twenty years had passed, yet that childhood incident was powerfully fresh and painful.

I grew up in the Seattle area and have been a Washington resident nearly all of my life. It wasn't until I was in college, however, in the 1970s, that I learned about the Japanese incarceration. How could I have grown up in an area where thousands of residents had been forced from their homes without being aware of it? I was shocked, and began reading about this shameful time in American history on my own. About a year ago, I heard the story of Pastor Emery "Andy" Andrews, who moved from Seattle to Twin Falls, Idaho, to be near his congregation, all of whom had been incarcerated in Minidoka. Though his course of action was terribly hard on his family, I was in awe of his courage and commitment. He didn't get caught up in the mob mentality that swept our country after Pearl Harbor. He did what he believed was right, no matter what.

I don't know if I could ever be as brave as Pastor Andrews, but I do know that it gives me hope to read about people like him. Perhaps that's true for you, too. And that's why I wrote *this* story.

— Kirby Larson, Seattle, Washington

Kirby Larson is the acclaimed author of the 2007 Newbery Honor Book *Hattie Big Sky*. She has also collaborated with Mary Nethery on two picture books — *Two Bobbies: A True Story of Hurricane Katrina, Friendship, and Survival*, which won the ASPCA Henry Bergh Award and the SIBA Book Award; and *Nubs: The True Story of a Mutt, a Marine & A Miracle*, a *New York Times* bestseller and a Christopher Award winner. Kirby lives in Seattle, Washington.

Acknowledgments

Though mine is the only name on the cover, there are many people who helped this book come into being. I am especially grateful to Brooks Andrews for sharing his father's story (and lending me many books!). Pastor Emery "Andy" Andrews and his caring and courageous actions were the inspiration for this story. Thanks, too, to Tom Light for talking with me about his experiences as a young boy at Minidoka; to Dee Goto for setting me straight about whether to use the term "interned" or "incarcerated"; to my nephew, Cody Miltenberger, for research assistance; to Lee Biggerstaff, Robert Colson, and Jack Glass, all of whom served on the USS *Enterprise* during WWII and were willing to help me understand many facets of life on board; to Eleanor Toews, Archivist at the Seattle Public Schools; and to Gloria Shigeno, who generously lent a complete stranger her precious copy of the *Minidoka Interlude*, the camp yearbook. Heartfelt thanks, too, to the people behind the Densho Project (www.densho.org), who are working feverishly to record the stories of the World War II incarcerees before it is too late.

Finally, thanks to Lisa Sandell, who is lovely inside and out and patiently pushed me to fill in the blanks; to Jill Grinberg, über-agent and miracle worker; and to all the patient early readers — Bonny Becker, Kathryn Galbraith, Sylvie Hossack, Helen Ketteman, Ann Whitford Paul, and especially David Patneaude, who helped me find a happier ending for Piper's story. And I would be nowhere without Neil Larson and Mary Nethery, who are the best team of cheerleaders any writer could want.

Grateful acknowledgment is made for permission to use the following:

Cover portrait by Tim O'Brien.

Cover background: Granger Collection, NY.

Page 300 (top): Japanese aerial photo of Pearl Harbor, Naval Historical Foundation.

Page 300 (bottom): A small boat rescuing a seaman from the burning USS *West Virginia* in Pearl Harbor, neg. #80-G-19930/National Archives.

Page 301: Loose Lips Might Sink Ships poster, neg. #NA 44-PA-82/ National Archives.

Page 302 (top): Victory garden poster, neg. #NA 44-PA-368/National Archives.

Page 302 (bottom): Victory gardeners, Corbis.

Page 303 (top): Soldier and Nisei posting Civilian Exclusion Order No. 1, neg. #PI-28038, Seattle Museum of History & Industry.

Page 303 (bottom): Instructions to All Persons of Japanese Ancestry, courtesy of the Yamada Family Collection, Densho: The Japanese American Legacy Project, www.densho.org.

Page 304 (top): Japantown boarded up, neg. #PI-28068/Seattle Museum of History & Industry.

Page 304 (bottom): Envelopes, courtesy of the Yamada Family Collection, Densho: The Japanese American Legacy Project, www.densho.org.

Page 305 (top): Hand-drawn map of Minidoka incarceration camp, Special Collections, University of Washington Libraries.

Page 305 (bottom): A panoramic view of the Minidoka incarceration camp, neg. #210-G-D106/National Archives.

Page 306 (top): A row of barracks, neg. #210-G-G413/National Archives.

Page 306 (bottom): Interior of incarceree's barrack apartment, *Seattle Post-Intelligencer* Collection, #86.5 (1), Seattle Museum of History & Industry.

Page 307 (top): Incarcerees preparing for Christmas, courtesy of Densho: The Japanese American Legacy Project, www.densho.org.

Page 307 (bottom): Incarcerees looking at the camp's honor roll, courtesy of the Mitsuoka Family Collection, Densho: The Japanese American Legacy Project, www.densho.org.

Page 308 (top): The Blue Box, courtesy of Brooks Andrews.

Page 308 (bottom): Map by Jim McMahon.

Other books in the
Dear America series

The Winter of Red Snow
The Diary of Abigail Jane Stewart
by Kristiana Gregory

A Journey to the New World
The Diary of Remember Patience Whipple
by Kathryn Lasky

Voyage on the Great Titanic
The Diary of Margaret Ann Brady
by Ellen Emerson White